BOOMER

A Memoir

Robert Docherty

PREFACE

Every generation blames the one before, but not me. I truly believe that they dealt with things as they saw fit in a less sophisticated world than the one I experienced. That said, I knew early on that I didn't want to live like they did. As a Boomer, like every generation, I rebelled against the norms of those who came before. People called it rebellion, but to me, it was simply living life and dealing with it on my own terms. So, my story is one of defiance and pushing boundaries.

I am calling this book a memoir because I want to take the reader on a journey through my childhood and travels. It is not a history book, although it is told in chronological order. Instead, I chose to highlight meaningful moments—selected events that shaped my life and travel. Life is built on moments: some I seized, others I let pass by. Together, these moments tell my story, crafted here with as few words as possible.

As I start this book, I am 77 years old. It is Matariki, and I am well and truly in the Drop Zone. Every morning, I wake up and think, *"I'm still here."* Many of my mates have already passed, and in 20 years, my entire generation will be gone. What I do know is that the world I grew up in no longer exists, and the life I lived is no longer an option for many. Through this memoir, I hope to show that even with little financial means, a person can live a life that is adventurous, meaningful, and worthwhile.

There is a cathartic aspect to this writing as I relive my childhood and travels. It's not quite a day of judgment, but I can see where I made mistakes and where I might have done better. Still, as Edith Piaf sang, *Non, je ne regrette rien.* What's the point of regrets? The two forces that motivated my life were survival and fun. I carried this attitude into my travels, and it shaped everything I did.

Boomers, in my opinion, have been judged harshly. We are accused of being wasteful, lucky, and contributors to the planet's decline. While there may be truth in the "lucky" label, I refute the accusations of wastefulness and responsibility for environmental degradation. Overpopulation, the burning of fossil fuels, and capitalist greed are the real culprits. I just wanted to have a good time—and I did. As I approach the end of my days, I'm not a rich man materially, but I am rich in experiences. My life is full of stories, which I will now share with you.

We Boomers grew up in a world recovering from war, where mentalities were still shaped by wartime discipline. Our fathers and mothers had endured incredible hardships. My father fought with the British Army and was wounded at both Dunkirk and the D-Day invasion. He lost many mates. Once, when I was six or seven, a car backfired in Lyttelton, and my father hit the deck in seconds. I stood there confused, not yet understanding what had shaped that reaction. My mother had been in the Land Army and lost her first love to the war. They emigrated from Scotland to New Zealand, hoping to leave those painful memories behind.

New Zealand, too, was still emerging from its war-induced hangover. Many veterans married, had children, and applied the army's strict disciplinary style to family life. A good clip across the earhole—or worse—was standard practice for many. Although my family was not like this, most of my schoolmates were regularly subjected to beatings. Women, having missed their men during the war, often pandered to them in ways rare today. This was the norm in the 1950s, but it all changed dramatically during the social revolution of the 1960s. We Boomers were at the heart of that change.

Schools mirrored the rigidity of society, emphasizing strict routines and discipline. Corporal punishment was common, especially in primary schools dominated by male teachers. I was strapped in primary school and caned three times in high school, mostly for trivial offenses. These experiences instilled a fear of authority, the law, and the police. Yet, alongside that fear, they bred resentment—a resentment that drove my rebellion.

We Boomer children pushed our parents to their limits, demanding change and freedom. We grew our hair long, wore bell-bottom trousers, and embraced the revolutionary music of the time. Starting with Bill Haley, Elvis Presley, Buddy Holly, and Chuck Berry, the music evolved into the incredible sounds of The Beatles, The Rolling Stones, Bob Dylan, and a host of other transformative artists. It was a musical renaissance, one that modern music struggles to replicate.

There was also a unique egalitarianism in New Zealand—a belief in giving everyone a fair go. The social, economic, and political gaps were far narrower than today. The Welfare State protected us from cradle to grave. Its dismantling remains, in my view, one of the greatest disasters of my lifetime.

New Zealand was a "pavlova paradise." Jobs were plentiful, and it was easy to make a living. The Trade Unions safeguarded workers, ensuring fair treatment. That sense of security and community is now gone. New Zealand has become a harder, more divisive society where inequality is stark, and politics only exacerbates it.

We also lived under the shadow of international tensions, with Communism and Western Capitalism locked in a Cold War. The Cuban Missile Crisis brought us to the brink of nuclear disaster, and the Vietnam War divided society like no other conflict. We marched in the streets, protesting for peace and sometimes cruelly abusing returning soldiers. It was a turbulent time, but our desire for peace was genuine.

The planet was still relatively pristine. We didn't think about climate change, pollution, or rising sea levels. The world was our oyster, open for exploration—everywhere except Communist China and the Soviet Union. Travel was a rite of passage, and we embraced it wholeheartedly. Our parents spoke of the "Old Country" with nostalgia, and thousands of us set off for London, crammed into ships. We endured meager lifestyles in the city before taking to Europe in Combi vans or hitchhiking. Between 1967 and 1975, I traveled across five continents as cheaply as possible. These journeys form the heart of my story.

My boomer upbringing, for all its flaws, gave me the resilience and skills to achieve these adventures. Afterwards, I settled into marital life, raised a family, built a career, paid my taxes, and waited for the so-called rewards of old age. I've reached that stage now, and looking back, it feels as though it all went by in a flash. I hope you enjoy these memoirs as much as I've enjoyed living the life they recount.

CONTENTS

PART 1:
GROWING UP

BEGINNINGS

I was born in Paisley, Renfrewshire, Scotland, in 1947. In 2004, my wife and I returned there. After walking around for a day, I said to myself, "Thank heavens my mother and father decided to leave and go to New Zealand."

My family roots were in Ireland on my father's side—the O'Dohertys—who left Ireland during the potato famine and changed the spelling of their name to Docherty. My great-great-grandfather and his kin lived in caravan-like gypsies, and I owe my wanderlust to them. On my mother's side, we were of the Douglas clan, the blue tartan. She was of the middle class. My mother attended a private school, learned the piano, and, along with her older sister Rachel and younger sister Margaret, worked in the family shop. Her father had been wounded in World War I and had a hole in his back that required daily dressing. When he died early, my grandmother developed paralysis and never walked again.

My father, Robert Townsley Docherty, was a boilermaker by trade and worked in the shipyards before the war. The war took a terrible toll on his life—a fact I never understood as a boy. Fathers and sons often have unspoken distances, and ours was no exception. He came from a Roman Catholic family of 14 children. I cannot recall meeting any of them, nor do I remember meeting my paternal grandparents. In fact, he rarely talked about his family, except for one incident at school, which was run by nuns. He had been unhappy with the treatment given to his younger brother Patrick and had pushed a nun to the ground. This act ended his formal education and resulted in his excommunication from the Catholic Church. It haunted him for the rest of his days, which was a shame because he was a deep thinker, read philosophy, and clearly could have pursued higher education. Then came the war—and what the nun had started, the war finished.

He joined the Seaforth Highlanders, a regiment allied with the Campbell clan. His first action with them was in Belgium and France, where they tried to deter Hitler's invasion. Of course, it failed. He was at Dunkirk, and the only thing he ever told me about it was that it was chaos—German aircraft strafing and bombing the beach. A bullet struck him in the shoulder, and he waited days to be evacuated. He never returned as a soldier until D-Day, when he was wounded again. On an advanced patrol seeking German positions, he walked into a German patrol. A brutal battle followed; many of his mates were killed, and he crawled away with a bullet in his buttocks.

He never spoke of the war—none of the men who fought did—but its shadow loomed over his life. The stress must have been terrible. I didn't understand this as a boy, and I marvel at how he coped with all he endured while raising eight children. It's something I only came to appreciate much later in life.

My mother, Helen Laurie Pettigrew Gourlie Douglas, married my father after he was demobbed in 1946. She was a vivacious woman who was the greatest influence in my life. My greatest regret is that I missed her last days and death because I was away from home working. Some of my brothers and sisters held this against me, as though it had been a deliberate choice, but I let that resentment go long ago.

When I was born prematurely in 1947, Scotland was still in war mode. Rationing was still in force and would remain so until 1951. Glasgow and its surrounding areas had been bombed during the war, especially the shipyards, and life was grim. People queued for food and supplies, and housing was harsh. My earliest memory is from around four years old. My father and I had gone to collect milk, which was ladled into cans that resembled paint tins. Silly me, I wanted to carry it—and spilled it everywhere. My father was angry, and the shock of that moment has stayed with me for life.

The grimness of post-war Scotland drove my grandmother and aunts, Rachel and Margaret, to emigrate to New Zealand, where they settled in Dunedin. This idea took root in my parents' minds, but my mother's pregnancy with my brother John delayed them. After John's birth, my father continued as a boilermaker and became a qualified tradesman. He applied for a job with Aulsebrooks in Christchurch, New Zealand, which he got. The company agreed to pay for our family's passage. However, another pregnancy postponed the plans again. In the end, urgency from the employer meant my father traveled ahead with just me and my three-year-old brother, John. We took passage on the *Port Dunedin* bound for Lyttelton.

The voyage was memorable for two reasons. Firstly, the ritual of being christened by King Neptune when we crossed the equator was a highlight, and I received a certificate to commemorate the feat. I often wondered what happened to that certificate in later years. Like much family memorabilia, it vanished without a trace, though I recall seeing it when we lived on Halberg Street in Dallington. The second memorable moment came when my father caught a shark off the stern of the ship using a butcher's hook, rope, and a lump of meat. It was pulled onboard and thrashed wildly around the deck. My father took some of its teeth as keepsakes. I saw them again at Halberg Street, but they, too, disappeared over time.

I was five years old when we arrived in Lyttelton in 1952. My father was lauded by the *Lyttelton Times* for bringing two young boys to New Zealand alone. We disembarked wearing kilts, and our photo appeared in the paper.

Lyttelton became our home for a couple of years. We lived in an old bungalow on Reserve Terrace near the cemetery. I was old enough to attend school but didn't, as my father had to work at Aulsebrooks. My aunt Margaret, likely no more than 17 at the time, cared for John and me. I remember her as a lively, spirited woman. My brother John shared at her funeral, when she was nearly 80, that he had thought she was his mother during those years. That belief changed, of course, when my mother arrived on the *Empire Star* with our new baby brother, Drew.

It was 1953 when I started school at Lyttelton Main School. Every day, I walked down Reserve Terrace, descending the jail steps to reach the school. My first day still haunts me. The woman teacher frightened me, and no one could understand what I was saying because of my broad Scottish accent. That accent lingered until I attended Burwood School in the mid-1950s.

Lyttelton held both happy and sad memories for me. My parents got me a dog named Lassie, a black-and-white collie, and we were inseparable. She would chase after me when I left for school and faithfully waited for my return after 3:00 p.m. Tragedy struck one day when she ran out and was hit by a rare passing motor car on Reserve Terrace. I cried and cried, desperately trying to drag her into our house. She was buried in the front garden near a large oak tree, and I never forgot her. In 2023, my wife, Celia, and I visited Lyttelton with our granddaughters, Emily and Catherine. I took a walk alone up the jail steps to Reserve Terrace, searching for the house. I couldn't find it but paused at the spot where Lassie had been killed nearly 70 years before. It brought a tear to my eye.

That same year, 1953, marked the coronation of Elizabeth II. The streets of Lyttelton reflected the occasion with a grand archway leading to the port. All the schoolchildren received medals to celebrate the event. Sadly, like many pieces of my childhood memorabilia, mine disappeared. How I wish I still had it.

As the months passed, tension crept into our home. My grandmother, who was in a wheelchair, came to live with us and required constant care. While my mother was devoted to looking after her, it became increasingly difficult as she was pregnant again— this time with my brother David. But the children didn't stop there.

Soon after, my mother became pregnant again with our sister Helen. I remember telling her, "Too many wains in this house, Mum!" Looking back, I suppose I wasn't wrong.

Despite the challenges, I liked my grandmother. She often told me stories about the war and sang old songs like *Coming In on a Wing and a Prayer.* I can still remember the lines of that song. Granny would encourage us to sing along with her, and in the evenings, my father would play the squeeze box while we sang together. I loved those moments. Christmas that year was especially memorable. My father dressed up as Father Christmas, carrying a bag of presents slung over his shoulder. We also had stockings filled with fruit and sweets, and family gathered together.

One of the joys of living in Lyttelton was Corsair Bay. In the summer, we would take the ferry around to the bay, swim out to the raft, jump off the jetty, and walk back home. Today, sadly, the water is considered unfit for swimming.

Then came the train strike. The train that passed through the tunnel to Christchurch was Lyttelton's lifeline. My father relied on it to get to work at Aulsebrooks. Without strike pay, he had no choice but to walk over the Bridle Path to Heathcote every morning and catch a bus into Christchurch. It's hard to imagine people doing that today, but back then, resilience was simply a way of life.

By 1955, the strike, my mother's pregnancies, five children, and my grandmother's care needs made life at home tense. We had to move. Eventually, we relocated to Harewood Camp, out by the airport. My grandmother went to live with my Aunt Rachel, a decision that caused acrimony within the family and lingering tension for years. I didn't see my grandmother again until I was ten and we had moved to Dallington. But before Dallington, there was Harewood Camp.

HAREWOOD CAMP

Harewood Camp was really a stopover accommodation for families waiting to get into a state house. We lived in a welfare state that looked after people from cradle to grave, and one of the goals was for everyone to live in a house and have an opportunity to get on their feet until they could buy their own. Some very famous people have come from state houses and been given their start in life by living in one, only to forget their roots when in positions of power and influence.

John Key falls into this category. We stayed in a flat numbered A4 and shared an entrance with A3, which was occupied by the Day family. The only thing I remember about them was that Mr. Day had all his teeth out in preparation for false teeth, and I remember his bloody grin when he showed me. I never understood the need to have all your teeth out, but many adults did it, including my own parents.

A4 was a small, cold flat with tar paper lining the walls. We were all crammed into three small bedrooms, with the bathroom and toilet at the end of an unlined hallway. Yet, it was home. When my sister Jeanette arrived, we shifted to another flat, W2, where we stayed until we got the call from State Advances telling us we had a house in Dallington—but that is another story. I do, however, remember the day we moved into W2 because we got new beds with large bed springs. They were set up in a large bedroom that was meant to bed the four boys—myself, John, Drew, and David. We were to share a bedroom here and at our next home for the next ten years. No privacy, no secrets. On this first day, however, like kids always do, we jumped up and down on the springs of the beds, which created hollows in the middle. This made sleep awkward, and we had to endure our folly for the next ten years.

For me, Harewood Camp was about the freedom I had to explore my world without adult interference. My mother was to have another child at this camp—my sister Jeanette—and we now had six children, which bore heavily on my parents, particularly my mother. "Go outside and play" was a familiar command from my parents, so outside we went. There was nothing inside to keep us indoors—no TV, no phone, no radio. We had books, of course, but we saved that for rainy days and night-time. So we explored, and what a playground Harewood Airport and its surroundings were.

My brother John and I became quite a team, which was to last through our teens until work, university, travel, and women whittled the relationship away. We often walked over to the airport, past the big water tower that marked the entrance. The airport terminal was very small, and there were few flights, but we saw the DC3s take off and land and later the DC4s, Globemasters, and Constellations as the airport got busier. The airport was shared by the aero club, with its array of small planes, and John and I used to hang around watching the men play with their toys.

To the south of the airport, where the Brevet Club now stands on Memorial Avenue, there was a dump and pastureland where we built imaginary worlds. We chased rainbows, built forts, climbed trees, threw stones, and played games. We were gone all day until hunger drew us home, and our parents never had to worry about what we were up to. We were responsible for ourselves, and at the time, we never thought of the dangers that people now fear for their children.

John and I were adventurous. At the back of our W2 flat, there was a creek, which we decided to dam. We collected stones and an old canvas sheet and built the sort of dam a beaver would be proud of, totally unaware of what the consequences would be. The dam worked a treat, and the adjoining paddock became a lake over two feet deep. We had found two half-oil drums—one tinted blue, the other red. We called them Bluebird and Redbird, and we paddled them through our lake, creating pirate fantasies as we went. It was brilliant until the authorities started to wonder about where and why the paddock was flooded. We were perceptive kids and heard talk in the shop about who could possibly have built the dam. So we never went back, stayed silent, and directed our attentions elsewhere.

There were two other outstanding features about Harewood Camp that brought us great joy. The first was a picture theatre, which showed film serials and cartoons every Saturday afternoon for kids, and a swimming pool where I learned to swim—a skill I now use every day in my old age. The movies were incredible, and it was here that I saw *The Wizard of Oz* for the first time and was smitten forever. John and I got a shilling every Saturday afternoon, and we bought 9d seats in the first three rows, spending the remaining 3d on an ice cream. This was true bliss. There was the occasional cartoon, and this was where Daffy Duck became my personal favourite. I wish I had a dollar for every time I said, "Thith means war." My favourite part was the serial that played before the main feature. I remember a series called *G-Men* and another series that eludes me now, with a villain called The Skull. After the movie, we would recreate what we saw in our play, and I always wanted to be The Skull.

The swimming pool in summer was a treat, and I learned to swim doing the breaststroke because this is what my mother and father did. Dad had been wounded in the shoulder in WWII and couldn't do the crawl, so I never did it, either. Remarkably, I still don't.

John and I—and later Drew—went to Harewood Camp School, and this was where I first learned of New Zealanders' obsession with rugby. It was the end of 1956, and the Springbok Tour had taken place. All the boys played rugby in the playground, and you were a sissy if you didn't, so I learned to play and realised I could play quite well. The school had Mr. Arnold as headmaster, and his son Dereck attended the school. Dereck was later to become an All Black. He was older than me and a bit of a bully, so I stayed well clear. I realised as early as this that I was a runner, not a fighter, and it has stood me in good stead ever since.

The question of religion raised its ugly head at the camp, and it disturbed me right from the start. Dad was a Catholic, and Mum a Presbyterian. None of us kids had been baptised, and both parents wanted us done. When they told us what was going to happen, I was immediately cynical and didn't want it to happen. A minister from St. Stephen's Church in Bryndwr came around and explained the process, and for the first time in my life, I was frightened. My parents were determined, and one Sunday, we all got picked up, taken to church, and one after another, had our heads anointed with water by the minister, who was a sickly-looking man. I took out my handkerchief and wiped the water off to the glares of those around me. That set the tone for my attitude towards religion from that day onwards.

The ugliest part of growing up in Harewood Camp was the school dental system. The country subjected us children to school dental nurses who drilled our teeth relentlessly without any evidence that there was anything wrong with them. In our family, there was little sugar in our diet, yet my teeth were massacred by the dental nurses at Fendalton School. We called it the "Murder House" as the nurse foot-pedalled drills and filled our teeth with amalgam. It wasn't until I received treatment from real dentists that my teeth were corrected, but only after two ruined teeth were pulled out. I will never forgive the system that allowed this to happen.

By 1957, change was on the way. We got a state house and moved to 15 Halberg Street, Dallington. I was sad to leave Harewood Camp behind—I had enjoyed life there.

DALLINGTON

Moving to 15 Halberg Street was the last move for my family, and it was here that I learned everything that was to affect what I did and felt for the rest of my life. I learned to cook, darn socks, mend punctures in my bike tyres, look after the meals while my very tired mother got some rest, and take my younger siblings to the doctor—many things that parents usually do. I was the eldest son and was expected to take responsibility when my father and mother worked. I was good at it, but it often meant disciplining my younger siblings, which they hated, and this often reflected in my relationships with them ever since.

It was here that the last two children, Alan and Brian, were born, bringing the number of kids to eight, and it was now no longer possible for us to live on my father's wage plus the family benefit. Mum had to work, and she knew it—and she did.

The house was a three-bedroom house with a sunroom, so the four boys, including myself, were put in one room, the two girls were put in another, and when the last two came, they were temporarily put in the sunroom. Later, this was reconstructed so that the four youngest boys were in one room, the girls in another, and John and I moved to the sunroom. It stayed that way until I left home when I was 18 and at university. It was a very cold house, and every winter's day, there was ice on the inside of the windows. There was no insulation in the walls, roof, or under the floor. My father used to light a fire every morning while us kids hovered around the oven in the kitchen to keep warm.

We were never hungry and went through four quarts of milk a day, three loaves of bread, and ate plenty of potatoes and mince. Many of the meals were cooked by me, as my father was at work, and my mother used to rise at 3 o'clock in the morning to go to work as a cleaner at the Post Office in the city. She was tired and needed rest, and the onus fell on me as the oldest son. Many of the younger members of my family never appreciated that, and it has reflected in our adult relationships ever since.

At the age of 11, I realised we were poor and had few possessions that other families had. I accepted that reluctantly. We had no car for a long time until we got an Austen 7, then a Ford V8, and later a Morris Oxford. If I wanted anything, I knew I had to work—so I did. I got a job as a paperboy for the *Star Sun* and did two rounds every day except Sunday, when there was no paper, and I collected paper subscriptions on Saturday mornings. For this, I got the princely sum of one pound a week, half of which I had to pay to my parents. The other half, I had to bank so that I could get my clothes, and I was allowed half a crown to spend on myself. I accepted this without argument because often, on a Friday, when I got paid and handed over ten shillings to my mother, it was the only money she had in her pocket. I did this for three years until I went to high school, and it was never known by the younger members of my family, who have, at times, judged me harshly. What I will say about family life is my parents were brilliant. Other kids who came around loved our parents, and unfortunately, many of my mates were regularly beaten by their fathers or their mothers. That never happened to me.

After leaving the paper round because of high school, I continued working with my brother John at market gardens near our home. We picked potatoes on frosty mornings, hoed rows of strawberries, and did other work, mostly for a lovely man called Mr. Bellingham. He paid us $2 a day, and this went into helping to provide our clothes and allowed my parents to stretch the budget further.

The freedom to wander was still a major feature of my life. After we received bicycles for Christmas, we extended our exploration to every corner of our city. There was nowhere we didn't explore—over to Sumner, out to the Waimak Bridge, into the city—everywhere. Our parents didn't worry, and we felt safe. Try doing that these days.

The greatest part of my life during this period was sports. I discovered that playing sport and keeping fit was one of the secrets of life, and I have done it all my life. We were lucky that next door to our house was a paddock that we used as our sports ground. We could play cricket and rugby all day with the neighbourhood kids—and we did so. Some games went on all day and were only interrupted by our mother calling us in for tea. You don't see that anymore.

Sport also gave us entry into all the games of national and international cricket and rugby at Lancaster Park. If you played sport, you got a red card, which allowed free entry, and my brother John and I used it whenever we could. One of my fondest memories is the third test between the British Isles Lions and the All Blacks in 1959. Nearly 60,000 people were at Lancaster Park, and the only way John and I could see the game was by hanging onto the back fence of the embankment. We saw Ralph Caulton score a brilliant try in the left corner, almost in front of where we were hanging. How we didn't fall still amazes me. We also saw cricket games, and I remember NZ, captained by John Reid, playing the English after an Ashes series against the Aussies, with Fred Trueman and Brian Statham opening the bowling for England. Fantastic.

When we got our first radio, it changed my whole way of thinking. We listened to programs like *The Goons, The Navy Lark, Around the Horn, Life with Dexter, Happy Hill, Night Beat,* and others. I don't think I ever looked forward to TV programs the way I looked forward to radio shows. The radio also brought popular music into our lives, and we listened to the Hit Parade every week and rock shows after school. *Elvis's Don't Be Cruel,* Ray Charles's *I Can't Stop Loving You,* and later, the hits of the Beatles and Stones became staples. We didn't get a TV until well into the '60s because they were so expensive, and we were lucky to watch some programs at our neighbours' across the street, the Lyons. Lex became one of our firm friends, and his father, Curley, was one of the best adults I had met in my life.

SCHOOLS AND EDUCATION

Lyttelton Main School was my first school, and it was here my learning began. A famous Scotsman, Sean Connery, once said that he got his biggest break at the age of five when his mother taught him how to read. Lyttelton did that for me. Because I had so much difficulty communicating with the other kids in my class because of my accent, I concentrated my energies on reading and rapidly moved through the books I was given, progressing well ahead of my class. I would take my given book home, read it to the end with my mother, and want another one the next day at school. This passion for reading stayed with me throughout my primary school years, and my parents encouraged me and my brothers and sisters by giving us books as presents at Christmas. My father was a prolific reader, as was my mother, and it was she who later introduced me to Agatha Christie. I recall reading all her novels throughout my childhood. Reading was to become an important part of my later life when I became an expert in children's literature, selected titles for the Schools Collection of the National Library, and promoted reading in schools. The seeds of this passion were sown in my first year of school at Lyttelton, so I owe a lot to Lyttelton Main School.

Harewood Camp School was different. Learning in school was done in a rote fashion. We recited the times tables until we knew them backwards, took words home to learn their meanings and spellings, and were tested the next day. Our teacher always read us a book, and we had silent reading every day.

Burwood School continued in the same fashion as Harewood but was more enjoyable because the teachers were brilliant. I was in Standard 3 (Year 4) when I went to Burwood, and my teacher was Mrs. Baxter. She seemed to like me and my accent and often got me to read aloud to the class. I was a very shy boy then, and other kids would rib me for it. Year 5 under Mr. Ford was much better. The discipline brought by a male teacher was heartening, and my learning took off again. Mr. Ford was a short-tempered teacher and used to throw chalk at people who weren't paying attention, but he read us some of the most amazing books I had ever read in my life. He began with *The Hobbit,* which drew me into a fantasy world that has stayed with me for the rest of my life.

Standards 5 and 6 (Years 7 and 8) were a treat for me. My teachers, Mr. Wilson and Mr. Sutherland, were strong disciplinarians, and like Mr. Ford before them, they both used the strap with some relish. Bad behaviour was solved with three of the best—or six of the best if you were really bad. This fear factor kept us in line, and luckily, I was never strapped at primary school.

At the end of Standard 6 (Year 8), I was second in the class behind a boy called Bernard Banks. The two of us, who had been accepted by Shirley Boys' High, were involved in a pilot scheme run by the high school. In this scheme, top students from the area, including Shirley Intermediate and other schools, were formed into a class that once a week spent half a day at Shirley Boys' learning French and Maths. When we went to Shirley Boys' full-time the following year, we became 3A, the top class doing Professional Studies at the school. I progressed with this class through the third, fourth, and fifth forms until after the School Certificate, when the University Entrance divided the class into specialist subjects.

Shirley Boys' High School was a brutal school full of boys who were finding their place. The teachers were equally harsh and ruled through fear of the cane. I was caned three times by three different teachers—and didn't deserve it. This experience made me resentful, and I lost respect for them, but my academic progress blossomed. By the end of my career at Shirley, I was probably about fourth or fifth in the school.

The story I must tell about my time at Shirley Boys' happened in

1964—the year of the Beatles. Everybody at Shirley was known by their surname, and there was a boy in my class called McEwin. He was different. Sometimes he was all smiles and extroverted behaviour; then, he would disappear into the class, and you never knew he was there. He loved the Beatles and brought a portable record player to school, playing their music at lunchtime. I used to join him, and we would sing and sometimes dance. When the Beatles came to town, there was no way I could go and see them—the money wasn't there. But McEwin asked me if I would go with him as he had two tickets. Of course, I said yes, but I couldn't tell anyone. On the night in question, I told my mother I had something on at school, wore my school uniform, and biked into the city, leaving my bike in the lane between Cathedral Square and Gloucester Street. McEwin was waiting for me outside the cathedral, and when I came, he grabbed my hand, and we walked to the Majestic Theatre.

It was bedlam—screaming girls everywhere. The Beatles came on in their light grey bum-freezer suits. Ringo was up on a high platform, John on the right, George on the left, and Paul in the centre. They began with *This Boy* and finished with *Twist and Shout*. They played for about three-quarters of an hour, bowed after every song, and then left quickly. The girls screamed the whole time. I got separated from McEwin, walked back to the Square, and biked home in the dark. I never told a soul. The next day at school, McEwin said nothing to me, so I left him to it. We hardly related from that day forward, and I never knew why. When I was at university, I was told that McEwin had died, and suicide was suspected. I never thought about it much, but on reflection, I think he was probably gay.

The best part of Shirley was the Friday morning assemblies, where we used to sing with the school brass band. Memorable songs were *Sussex by the Sea*, with all the boys singing "shussix shussix by the sea" after a favourite radio show character, Cecil Snipe, from a program called *Round the Horn*, who exaggerated his s's. Two teachers, Edmund Bowen and Mr. Robson, often sang at assembly, and a highlight was their rendition of the *Gendarmes' Duet*. These moments gave life to the otherwise drab school day.

The second-best part was sport, at which I was fairly good. I played one game for the First XV rugby team and one for the First XI cricket team before finding myself in the second team. I had incurred an injury to my knee while at Burwood, and it inhibited my commitment at times, so the coaches didn't want me in the top sides. Fair enough, but it hurt me. It wasn't until I was 61 years old that I discovered the injury to my left knee was a torn cruciate ligament—an injury that used to end careers in my day. But running had strengthened the muscles around the knee, and I was able to complete marathons and play cricket as a medium-paced bowler into my 60s. But that is another story.

The sorriest thing about leaving Shirley was that in the next two years, four of my former classmates committed suicide.

UNIVERSITY OF CANTERBURY

In a nutshell, I *hated* it.

I went to university thinking it was a place of freedom of ideas and learned very quickly, as I failed abysmally in my first year, that the only way to pass was to regurgitate your lecturer's ideas. So I did, and from then on, I passed everything. I did enjoy studying history, and it became my major subject, along with English and geography, in the B.A. that I completed in 1969.

I made few friends at university and largely avoided university events, preferring instead to go out drinking with my brother John and neighbours Wayne Whittaker and Lex Lyons. Our interest in music was greatly enhanced after we found a blues club called *The Stage Door* with the resident band, *The Chants*. They opened our ears to the blues, and it has been my favourite music ever since.

We had one experience that gave us an inkling of what fame must feel like for music stars when the Yardbirds came to town. Lex, Wayne, myself, and my brother Drew took a taxi to the Theatre Royal to see them. When we pulled up outside, the taxi was mobbed by girls. We were dressed in our colourful hippie gear, and they thought we were the band. Books and pens were thrust through the window, and I recall signing a few as Eric "Slowhand" Clapton. We told the taxi driver to drive around the block before walking back to the theatre. Our 15 minutes of fame—I loved it. The ironic thing is that Clapton had already left the Yardbirds, but they did bring two great guitarists with them: Jimmy Page, who played lead, and Jeff Beck, who astonishingly played bass.

In my last year at university, I did make one very good friend in Bill Stalker, a tall beanpole of a man who loved photography and acting. I accompanied Bill to many parties and plays produced at Canterbury

University, including one memorable production of *A Midsummer Night's Dream* directed by the great Ngaio Marsh. I helped out backstage but felt out of my depth with the after-play socialising. I seemed younger and less mature compared to these actors, so I often slipped away to *The Stage Door* and blues music. I later learned that Bill joined an entertainment group called *Blerta* with Bruno Lawrence and did the talking part on their hit record *Dance All Around the World*. Sadly, Bill met his death shortly after in a motor accident in Australia, but I still have photographs that he took during our friendship.

I did have an episode in my last year at university that I am not proud of, but it needs to be mentioned. I was having a relationship with a girl who was much younger than me, though you would never have known it. She had a child by me—a daughter—and I deserted her. I was given a chance to do something about it on the eve of my departure to Australia, but I chose not to. The little girl was adopted by a well-to-do family and had an upbringing that I could never have given her, but the guilt is still there. I am fortunate, however, that I now have a relationship with Sarah, as she looked me up in her 20s after the death of the man she called Dad.

My history degree had given me a lifelong interest in ancient civilisations and cultures, and I vowed that I would see the world of these cultures as soon as I possibly could. And I eventually would. Greek, Egyptian, Roman, Babylonian, Aztec, Inca, Mayan, and others would soon be in my grasp.

To get your degree in those days, you had to attend a capping function. I got a job labouring at Davis Gelatine, saved my money, and on the day after I graduated, I left for Australia, beginning six years of travel. I loved working at Davis Gelatine, where my foreman was a fabulous bloke called Frank Walsh, who died too soon in his early 70s. Frank gave me every chance, and I was able to make $40 a week with Saturday morning work. It was smelly work, but I lived at home for $10 a week, spent the same on entertainment, and banked

$20. You could go out with $2 in those days, get pissed, see a good band, and have a Chinese meal to boot. I built up a small hoard and bought a ticket on the *Angelina Lauro* to Sydney, leaving after my graduation in March 1970.

The capping ceremony was held in the King Edward Barracks in Christchurch, and my mother and sister Helen attended. The next day, I was on a ship to Sydney and couldn't have dreamed of the life I was about to have.

Next up is the second part of my story about my travels, the part I most wanted to write about.

Taken in 1953 when I arrived at Lyttelton New Zealand with my father and brother John.

Harewood School 1954. I am in the second row from the top two in from the teacher.

My class at Shirley Boy's High school. A bright but sad lot. Four suicides one yuear after school.

My brothers and sisters with my mother centre. Left to right Brian, Alan, Drew, John, Me, David.Bottom Jeanette, Mum, Helen. A photo never to be taken again.

My father with Drew John, david, Me and Brian getting pissed at
home 1966.

The Stage Door 1966 with Wayne, Lex, John and me 1966.

Some of the best days of my life.

23

University Capping Week 1969.L-R Warren Pullar, Craig Ashley, Me, Donna, Bill Stalker.

PART 2:
TRAVELING THE WORLD

A confession that I must make before I start talking about my journey around the world, where I visited all continents except Antarctica, is that I had no plan.

I made it up as I went along, and most of what I did occurred by chance. A chance meeting, a chance thought, a chance opportunity, or a forced option. I was a loner, although at times I traveled with people, but generally not for long. And most importantly, I was a traveler, not a tourist. I did some tourist things, but travel was my business.

I had a fascination for historical cultures that had gotten humankind to where it ended up, and I wanted to see these for myself. But there was always the question of money. I wasn't a rich man, I wasn't even a poor man, but I was a wandering soul, and I knew that there were things out there that I had to do before I left this mortal coil. My childhood had given me all the skills I needed to survive, and my education had given me an organized mind. I was ready to try the world, and what better and most obvious place to start than Australia?

I had been to Australia during the university holidays of 1968/69, traveling by ship across the Tasman to Sydney and hitchhiking to the city. A bit of work on a building site, then to the Gold Coast, sleeping on the beach and boozing up when I could. I ran out of money, of course, hitched to Sydney again and threw myself at the mercy of the Salvation Army, who got me a job with a working gang laying cables in North Sydney. I learned the layout of Sydney, and doing the manual shovel work suited me while, at night, bedding down in a single man's hostel.

I carried everything I had with me in a backpack and took it to work every day. People in missions are thieves, and anything you have is fair game to them. But I learned and got a good feel for Sydney and knew that I would be back. The biggest plus for Australia was the wages. I could earn more in a week in Australia than I could in a fortnight in New Zealand, and I believe it is still that way.

I arrived in Sydney at Easter, hung out at a boarding house in Kings Cross that I had found when last in Sydney, and on the Tuesday after Easter, went to apply for a job at the Post Master General's Dept, citing my degree as a reference for my abilities. They had nothing going but did have a job in a manhole building gang, and would I like it? And I bloody well did. Fortune had struck early, and I reported the next day to the gang leader, whose surname was the same as mine. Jimmy Docherty, an angry Scotsman who insisted I was related to him in some way. I hoped not, but if it kept me in employment, it was ok by me.

My first day at work was below the Sydney Harbour Bridge, in Lower Fort Street, and the job was digging a manhole for coaxial cables that the PMG dept was laying all over Sydney. This was to be my job— digging a manhole in the blue-red mudstone that lies beneath Sydney, then building a shell with Acrow panels around the hole, pouring concrete on it, fitting a manhole cover, and there you have it. I helped build dozens of them, most on the North Shore, which was a developing suburb in those days.

The work was hard, and I was often required to use a jackhammer to chip away at the mudstone to about the same depth as a grave and then build the cover around it. No ear muffs in those days, and I regret that I paid the price with a loss of hearing in my later years. I enjoyed the work and made a great friend in an Italian immigrant called Angelo. The Aussies used to give him gip, called him a "wog," and generally made his life hell, but I liked him, and he often shared his delicious lunch with me. The job was also good in that I could initially walk to work, and as the location of the holes changed and we worked on the Shore, I could catch a train to Chatswood Station, where Jimmy would pick me up and drop me off at the end of the day.

I did this for 3 months, working 6 days a week and the odd Sunday when I cleared $100-$120 a week. I lived off the smell of an oily rag, rarely went out, but when I did, I went whole hog. I recall going to a wine bar in Oxford Street where the band playing was a very young Little River Band. The music was terrific, and I had a skin full. I was kicking a tin can along the road when the cops stopped me and asked what I was doing. I said I was kicking a can along the road, to which they replied, "Don't get smart with us," and I spent the night in jail and had to pay $40 for the privilege. I was not amused, but it taught me a valuable lesson—not to come to the attention of the police or, for that matter, anyone official. I stuck with that, and it was very good advice.

While living in the Cross, which was the nightlife area of Sydney and was worked by prostitutes, pimps, drug dealers, and all sorts of riffraff, I encountered a couple of old acquaintances from Christchurch—Rod Caffin and Dave Barnes. Dave was one of the nicest guys I ever met, with a great sense of humor, and Rod was one of the best street conmen I ever met.

It was through them that I got to know about drugs. I had had the odd toke of Mary Jane in Christchurch, but it was very weak, and I got little from it. Rod had LSD, and my first and best trip was with them in the Cross. It was brilliant. The fountain was like a stairway to heaven, and we went to a club/restaurant called the Ball Pants, which had the Ivor Novello Awards on the television, in which a very young David Bowie, with long blond curly hair, was playing *Space Oddity* and I just tripped out of my mind. Although the experience was incredible, I couldn't afford to do this. I wanted to see the world, but Mary Jane, in particular, was to become a part of my life. I was becoming a hippy.

It was then that I read in the paper about a ship called the Southern Cross, which was going from Sydney via Auckland, Wellington, Lyttelton, Samoa, Fiji, Tahiti, Panama, Fort Lauderdale, Miami,

Bermuda, and then Southampton for the cost of about $300. I booked a passage, applied for a British passport, got my vaccinations, and worked out my notice on Jimmy's gang. He was not pleased and said I had a good future if I stayed, but there was no way I was staying. I was ready to take my chances in swinging London.

The voyage was seven weeks, and much happened, but at times, it was like being "idle as a painted ship upon a painted Ocean." The Pacific Ocean is enormous, but even staring at the sea from the deck, I saw small fishing boats, many flying fish, and mused at the scale of it all.

I was allocated a four-berth cabin with three other guys, and at times, it was testy, but I did meet an amazing guy called Johnnie Parsons, who was 14 years older than me but wilder than a den full of weasels. He had come off working in the iron mines of Western Australia, and I had been restricting myself socially in Sydney, working my ass off. We were both ready for a good time, and that's what we did. We drank every day and became friends with a bunch of Aussies who were to become our flatmates in East London at the end of the long voyage.

There was not much to do on board as there is on today's cruise ships, but we did play deck cricket using a rope ball, which didn't bounce much, and even had a test series—Australia v England—in which I played for England and won. But the highlight was, of course, the stops, where all manner of hell took place.

I had shoulder-length hair at this stage and wore a leather headband to keep it out of my eyes. People cottoned on to this on board, and I was known as Geronimo. I felt pressure to perform all the time. Looking back, I am ashamed of my behavior at this time; I was rude, disorderly, and out of control, and very lucky that nobody had beaten the shit out of me.

The port stops at Apia, Nandi, and Papeete were a continuation of my drunken shipboard antics, as Johnnie and I ripped it up in the portside bars. It wasn't until the journey from Tahiti to Panama that I settled down. The good reason for this was that the sea was pretty rough, and I felt sick, so I lay around on my bunk. It gave me 5 days off the booze, but Panama was to stir me up again. Panama City was a wild place, and me, Johnnie, and the Australians swaggered around trying to buy cocaine just to see what it was like. We encountered some pretty rough dudes and thought we had bought some for US$20, but it was crap stuff. The trip through the Panama Canal was a sight, and I suddenly became aware that there was a world to see. Another port stop at Fort Lauderdale took me back to a bar inside a converted Lancaster Bomber, but I was more circumspect with my drinking and behavior. The next stop was Bermuda, and this was a beautiful place. Instead of the bars, I hired a bike and pedaled around the island before a farewell drink at the Hog Penny. I was heartily sick of the ship and ready to face the UK.

We docked at Southampton 5 days later, caught a train up to London, and headed down to Johnnie Parsons' old haunt, Forest Gate, in the East End of **London**. We stayed a couple of days at a B'n'B and were having a drink in the Princess Alice boozer when we encountered a man called Krupa, who had a two-room house in Hampton Road to rent at ten quid each a week, so we moved in.

London life was about to begin, and it was a standard of living that was well short of what I was used to in New Zealand. We had no shower, just a bath where the water was heated by gas. Having a bath was quite an adventure and expensive, so I rarely bathed, and I had to do my washing in the laundromat about two blocks down on Romford Road.

We ate at the greasy spoon on Romford Road, where an unfortunate incident happened that still bewilders me. The diner had a jukebox, and the big song at the time was Max Romeo with *Wet Dream*. It was a reggae song and had suggestive lyrics, and when I put it on, a man took exception to it and tried to punch me out. I had good company, and the lads put him right, but it taught me to keep a low profile, and from then on, I did. Nobody likes a show-off in **England**, and a fight is never far away. I was a runner, not a fighter.

Xmas came around, and it snowed—the first in London since 1947, the year I was born. It was a white Xmas, and I was short of money and needed a job. I saw a sign up in Stratford that Ford was looking for workers, so I went for an interview. The jobs were on the assembly line, and the interviewers, though with my university degree, thought I was too qualified for the job and that they were interviewing later in the month for office staff, and I could come back then. I was bemused and left, walking around Stratford, where West Ham's ground at London Stadium now stands. I turned and walked back to talk to them again and said I was interested in the office job but felt that knowing what went on on the factory floor would help me understand Ford better. They were impressed, and I got to start on the following Monday. My relief was immense because I was almost broke.

Working on the assembly line at Ford was like a scene out of the Charlie Chaplin film *Modern Times*. There were two assembly lines making Cortinas at Dagenham: a slow line and a fast line. I was on the fast line. A line of engines would come into the area where I worked, and on a rail above the chassis would come. My job was to lower the chassis down to the engine with precision so that bolts could be inserted and the two parts joined. I stood on a platform behind the car, just done and the one to be done. I manipulated the lowering button to make the fit, and two guys on either side would push the bolts through, which I would then tighten with an air-compressed gun. The line never stopped unless there was an incident, and there were plenty of incidents. They slowed the line down for 10 minutes for morning tea and 10 minutes for afternoon tea, and lunchtimes were rostered so that the line kept going.

I did this for six months, working two weeks on days at about 26 pounds a week, then two weeks on nights at 32 pounds a week. There were times when I didn't know whether I was Arthur or Martha, but I got used to it as we had the weekends off, and I used it watching West Ham play football, as Upton Park was on Green Street, just down the road, and going to see bands.

Watching West Ham play was brilliant. They had Bobby Moore as captain and had such notable players as Geoff Hurst, Billy Bonds, Harry Redknapp, and Jimmy Greaves playing for them. If they were away to a London team, I would go watch them there. You had to be careful not to alert the opposition sides as to your allegiance, or a good kicking could result, but that wasn't my scene. Although many of the fans, known as the Inter City Firm, often caused havoc and were feared by many clubs. On one of the few times I went to an away game, which was at Leicester, the Inter City Firm kicked the shit out of the rail carriages, and when we arrived in Leicester, police on horseback prevented us from going anywhere except the game. It was the same at the end of the game. I never went away with the West Ham fans ever again. I preferred to make my own way and stay away from trouble.

After the games, or when West Ham were away, I would go see bands play. It was the beginning of Glam rock, with T. Rex, the big band. Bowie was just starting, and George Harrison had *My Sweet Lord* in the charts. Freda Payne had *Band of Gold* playing in every pub, but the band I liked was Dave Edmunds and Rockpile. They had an old Fats Domino song, *I Hear You Knocking*, in the charts, and later *Girls Talk*. I saw them playing up West, and it was brilliant. Every Thursday at 7:00, I would watch *Top of the Pops* at the local boozer, with Pan's People doing the naughty bits and the Top 20 countdown.

At this stage, I was living on my own in a bedsit, cooking my own meals, and working to save money to travel. Then Ford went on strike, and it lasted a month. I wasn't in the Union, although I did attend the meeting that voted by a show of hands and ayes to go on strike. They wanted an extra fiver a week, and management dug their toes in. Relationships between management and staff were not good, but the union guys did put continual pressure on them, and there were a lot of backhanders and jiggery-pokery going on, which I had no part in.

I anticipated that the strike would be long, so I went and got a job at a local firm that was making flues for heating and plumbing systems. It was hard work and poorly paid, but I needed the money, and it was all-day shift and within walking distance of my bedsit. I got on well with the guys who worked there, and we went to West Ham games together. It was very noisy, though, and I don't think it did my hearing any good at all.

Once the strike was over, I went back to Ford and had some very good luck. I had been on an emergency tax bracket, which was higher than the normal worker, and while on strike, my new tax code came through, and I received a 250 quid rebate on my first pay. The strike gave us an extra 3 quid. I was in the money, so I worked a further three weeks, and by the end of June 1971, summer was here, and I was ready to go.

But before that, I followed my other sporting passion, cricket, and went to see England play India at Lord's, which was brilliant. That was England for me. I packed my backpack, left my bedsit without paying, and got out on the road to hitchhike to Dover and a ferry to Europe. No plan—I was going wherever fate took me, and fate took me across Europe, through Turkey, Iran, Afghanistan, Pakistan, India, and on to Australia via Malaysia. A journey I had only dreamed of.

OVERLAND TO AUSTRALIA

While I was relying on fate to get me where I was going, I did vaguely have some sort of plan and knew that when I left England, I didn't immediately want to go back. Going overland was always my aim. Johnnie Parsons, my cabin mate on the *Southern Cross*, had stimulated my interest because he and three mates had driven a car to India from London and then moved to Australia. He told wild stories, and I thought to myself, "I am going to do that."

When I arrived at Ostend in Belgium off the Dover Ferry, I was ready for anything. My only guide was a map of Europe—no cellphone, no internet, no navigation system, just a map. This would be unheard of in the 2024 world I'm living in now, where everybody is connected every minute of the day.

I had just over 500 pounds on me in travellers' cheques, which nobody uses now, and a small number of low-denomination British pounds for emergency or small transactions. I kept a small amount in my pockets when I was traveling; the rest, along with my passport and vaccination certificate, was in a money belt with a leather pouch for the travel documents, which I wore under my clothes every minute of the day. In my pack, I had one good shirt, a pair of good Levi jeans, bell-bottomed, of course, a couple of T-shirts and singlets, two pairs of grundies, a good shirt to wear when crossing borders or going for visas (the East is very sensitive about these things, especially places like Malaysia and Singapore), a heavy jersey, a leather jacket, a strong pair of shoes, a pair of jandals, a groundsheet that doubled as a raincoat-type poncho, a woolly hat, two pairs of socks, a bag of toiletries, a swimming costume and shorts, a sleeping bag with an inner sheet that could be used as a sleeping bag in hot weather, a water bottle, a knife and fork, and an enamel plate (enamel plates are wonderful things), a torch (much coveted by thieves), and the clothes and gym boots that I stood up in. My camera and writing gear, plus a book, were on the outside of the pack in the pouches for easy access, along with a Swiss Army knife, which was needed all the time with its fabulous gadgets. I was ready for anything but a bit green and had a lot to learn.

The hippy thing had hit Europe, and there was a great vibe among travellers. The trail overland that I was heading for was called the hippy trail, and I always talked to backpackers to see where they had been, good cheap places to stay, places to change money, and any information that was valuable regarding borders, visas, transportation, etc. Traveling sounds like a simple, easy life, but my impression was if you treated it like that, you were done. Traveling was work, survival, something you did every day, and at the end of the day. Hopefully, you had a bed to sleep in, a good meal, and company. In my experience, that was not always the case, but what doesn't kill you makes you stronger, and the further I went, the stronger I got.

The first night in Ostend, I slept on the riverbank with a lot of other travellers and got up early to try to hitchhike out. What a surprise—the freeway out of Ostend was lined for about 300 meters with people like myself, and I was in a hurry to get things underway. I was always like this when I started travelling again; the first month couldn't go quick enough, so big decisions had to be made. I decided that I wasn't going to tour Europe, but I did want to see Roman and Greek culture and ruins, so I took a train to Luxembourg. I wanted to go here because I used to listen to Radio Luxembourg at night when living in my bedsit in London. I looked around for a day, then caught a train to Italy. It was overnight, so I could sleep on the train. Not a bad tactic when you're going a long distance, and I frequently took overnight trains and buses to roll away the miles.

On the train, I met a guy from Liverpool who was going to see his girlfriend, who lived in a Mediterranean town called Sori. We got on so well that I decided to join him, and it proved to be a good idea.

Sori was a little harbour where sardine boats left at night to catch their prey, and there was a shed on the beach where I could sleep at night, so I did. I stayed on Sori Beach for three days, and on the second night, I was asked if I wanted to go out fishing, so I said yes. It was a small boat with a big lamp on the back and a rubber dinghy in tow. We went out at about 7:00 p.m. into the Mediterranean until it got dark. On went the lamp, shining into the water, and one guy rowed out, feeding the fine-meshed net into the water as he went. Then we had a drink and slowly pulled out the net. It had many sardines in it, which we put into buckets, and then we returned home to the beach. Fantastic. The next night, we all had a meal, and I decided I should get off before I got too comfortable. I had a mission to accomplish, but I learned how good the simple life could be.

I started hitching early in the morning with no luck, so I took a bus to Rome—and what a city it was. Got a cheap pension, met a couple of American guys, and did the sights—Colosseum, the Forum, Spanish Steps, the catacombs, St. Peter's Square, etc.—and saw the greatness that had been the Roman Empire. Rome was expensive, and I was going through the money, so I had to take stock.

I walked out of Rome to the motorway south en route to Napoli, and was picked up by a truck driver, which proved to be my most memorable story of Italy. Before he let me in the truck, he asked me, "Do you like the Beatles?" I said yes, of course, so he let me in. All the way to Napoli, I had to sing Beatle songs, and it was brilliant. I threw in a few of my own versions, like "I'll never dance with her mother; I saw her standing there" and "Speaking words of wisdom, Lipton's tea." He was a great guy and took me to a cheap pension in Napoli, where I could gaze up at Mt. Vesuvius.

This had greatly heartened me, and I enjoyed going to Pompeii, but Napoli was rough and dirty, even though it sat on one of the best harbours I'd ever seen. I was in a hurry, however, and I wanted to get to Greece, so I got on the road to Brindisi, where I heard you could catch an overnight ferry to Patras, but I changed my mind. I was picked up by an American couple who were going to Corfu, and they waxed lyrical about it, so it was in Greece, and I knew the Duke of Edinburgh had been born there, and I had read a book by Gerald Durrell on Corfu, so I said, "What the hell," and caught the boat.

I wasn't disappointed—Kerkyra was a brilliant little town, and I could stay at the youth hostel there, sleeping outside with all the other hippies and travellers for a few drachmae a night. I stayed a week, swimming in the sea, smoking dope with everybody, talking shite, and listening to music. It was wonderful, but good things come to an end, and I caught the ferry to Patras, another overnighter, and slept on the deck with everybody else.

I planned to go straight to Athens but was picked up by a Mercedes, driven by a big man who was the driver/bodyguard of an attractive black girl from Switzerland. They were going to a hotel with private huts, and they asked me to stay. Of course, I said yes, but the bodyguard made it quite clear that the woman, who was about 18 or 19, was completely out of bounds. I agreed, basically because I assessed that she was out of my league. I planned to stay the night and had a few retzinas, which is a dry white wine, potent but absolutely bloody awful. I watched the Greek men dancing and breaking plates, and I was cool with that. Then the girl produced a joint, and we smoked it, and she began to get amorous, but I am afraid I was scared, made my excuses, grabbed my pack, and went back on the road. I got nowhere, of course, so I walked inland a short way and bedded down.

In the morning, I walked a ways, and off to my left emerged a magnificent spectacle called the Gulf of Corinth. It was a long way down, and there were ships passing through. I had read of Corinth in Greek history and caught a local bus into Corinth, where there was a garden with statues of naked men and women in various states of arousal. I thought whimsically of the night before but put it down to experience and looked for a hotel for the night.

I learned that it was possible to sleep on the roof of some Greek hotels cheaply, so I did that and talked to other travellers about Athens and where to eat and stay. The next morning, I took the local bus into Athens, found a cheap hotel where I could sleep on the roof, and over the next three days, I explored the wonders of Ancient Greece. The Acropolis was superb—I walked up to the top and wandered around all day. There was an amphitheatre at the side where plays were enacted, and music played. I shamelessly walked out and sang Elvis Presley's *It's Now or Never*, for which I received a half-hearted clap from someone. I was enjoying myself.

Up on the roof of the hotel, I met other travellers and discussed the Greek Islands, good ones to see, and where to catch the ferry at Piraeus. Many hippies were going to Ios and Patmos, but I wanted to go as close to Turkey as I could so that I was still going forward. So, I went to Samos. Byron had written about the wine from Samos, and somehow I had remembered this, and Samos Sec was a popular drink. On the ferry there, I met a German guy called Karl, and he wanted to sleep on the beach, so we got off the ferry and walked about half an hour out of town—and behold, a near-deserted beach. This suited me fine, so it became my home for the next week, and we were joined by other travellers, mostly German. There was plenty of dope around, but Karl was an alcoholic, and I was always willing, so we would walk into the town and drink. On one occasion, we went too far and stole a bicycle to get back. I pedalled, Karl was on the crossbar, and we sang songs all the way back. The next day, the police were around asking questions. I took my usual stance of knowing nothing, but it wasn't good form, and that afternoon, Karl and I were on the boat to Turkey.

The Turks and the Greeks were not good friends at the time, as something was going on in Cyprus, and there was a chance that we wouldn't be able to land, or so the captain told us. He was wrong, thankfully, and after finding a cheap hotel, we were ready to explore the ancient city of Ephesus the next morning. It was brilliant, but very hot, and that afternoon we took a local bus to Izmir, up the west coast, and en route to Istanbul.

There was no bridge across the Bosphorus in those days, but the ferry boat passed Topkapi Palace on the way, and we could see the Blue Mosque and Hagia Sophia rising above the city. Only Rio, for me, had a better harbour view. The Turks wouldn't let us stay on the roof, so we shared a room with four others with a cold shower. Dope smoking was out of the question, and the city itself had obvious dangers. Groups of young men and street hawkers were everywhere. Karl had become a liability, and I tried to shake him off by leaving early in the morning and exploring the fabulous city until dusk. I found a great pudding shop, which was to appear in the Billy Hayes film *Midnight Express*, and I met a Canadian guy named Don Fawcett, who was to become my travel companion for the next month. He was from Calgary and had a cowboy mentality, but I liked him, and it was his idea to give the rest of Turkey a miss and travel straight through to Tehran in Iran, so we bought a bus ticket for around $10 USD on a journey that would take four days.

Most of Turkey was not much to look at, mostly brown and barren. Ankara came and went, and we passed through a series of little villages where we saw only men and children, and if we saw a woman, she was dressed head to foot in hijab and full robes. In a large town called Erzincan, we saw how rapidly social and religious differences could be inflamed. The passengers on the bus were mainly Arab and Turkish, but there were at least 10 European travelers like myself and Don. There was one large American girl named Betty who was very well-endowed and bounced around with gay abandon—braless, of course—and when we stopped at a refreshment stop in Erzincan, some of the men took exception and started screaming at her and slapping her around. Everybody got on the bus rapidly, as did Betty in tears, and the driver wisely put the foot down as we sped out of town in a hail of abuse and stones. It was a warning never to forget: we were in their country.

As we got nearer the border, the roads got better, as is the case at most land borders, and there was no problem getting through. Iran put on its best show of opulence for about 50 km. Then it was the same barren landscape and run of small towns with the only obvious inhabitants being men and children, plus their livestock—sheep and goats. We got to Tehran in the morning, and it was a bustling modern city. It was the days when the Shah was in charge, and there was a distinct Western influence. Women in modern Western attire were on the street, and the strict Islamic attitudes were not as obvious, but Don and I were soon to find out how deceptive that was. Our main aim in Tehran was to get a visa to go to Afghanistan, so I swept back my hair, put on my best shirt (Don was already smart), and we visited the Afghan Embassy. They were good, but we needed six photographs, and I didn't ask why. The application asked some bizarre questions, like, "What was my grandmother's maiden name?" I made most of it up, and under "Occupation," I put "Poet." The photographs were not hard to get, but we had them done by a sort of box contraption, to which we stood two meters back while the photographer took off the lens cap for a couple of seconds. Then, there were some chemicals, and a grinning picture of ourselves resulted. We did this six times each, put them with the application and our passports, and left them overnight—or so we thought. It was Thursday and then Friday, which is the Muslim Sunday, so everything was closed. We had to stay in Tehran for another day and night at least. We found the bus station and found out about tickets to Mashad, a holy city near the border with Afghanistan, and planned our exit for Sunday.

We had found a cheap hotel with a cold-water shower, cleaned up, and decided to walk around Tehran. We visited the Shah's palace and weren't allowed to take photographs, but I secretly got one, and we walked past a nightclub with a bouncer outside beckoning us to come in. We thought about it and said "later" and went back to the hotel. I had managed to pick up some hash at the border, as did the other Westerners on the bus. We were targets everywhere for dope dealers. Don had never done hash before, and I was very new to it, but we had some and went back to the nightclub, walking on air. The bouncer was gone, but we went in, sat down, and ordered a drink—non-alcoholic, of course. The music was local stuff—lots of screeching drums and strings—but we were in their country, and when in Rome... Almost immediately, two local girls dressed like Westerners approached us and sat down. We thought they were prostitutes, but it seemed that they were not. They knew a little English, and there was a bit of laughter. Suddenly, two burly men came up, grabbed the girls, and started slapping them around, so Don and I got up and hurriedly left. The high from the hash started to spread in, and panic took over—we just ran.

The lesson of Turkey had not sunk in, but it had now. The next day we picked up our passports with visas, and the Afghan officer said, "You poet?" I said yes. "What you write about?" I said, "Life." He grinned and let me go. We stayed in our room the next day, getting stoned and reading and eating, and on Sunday, we went down to the bus station and took the bus to Mashad.

Mashad was nothing like Tehran, with the Muslim culture far more in evidence. This was not a place to stand out in, but the mosque was very beautiful. We found a hostel that was full of Western travelers, and there was a relaxed mood about the place, and the bonhomie that characterized the hippy trail was fully evident. There was laughter, flirting, music, and hash. Don and I had met a bus of hippies going to Kabul and on to India the next day, and of course, we asked if we could come with them. All was well, and it cost us nothing.

The road to the border was great, the border crossing easy, with the guards eager to sell us the famed Afghani hash—and they did good business. The hotel on the border boomed that night, but the dreaded lurgy struck most of the passengers and the driver down. I had gone to bed early because the hash was strong, and my head was saying, "Lie down," and I didn't eat the grapes that were around. The toilets were a popular place. The driver couldn't drive, and nobody else would do it, so it was down to Don or me if we wanted a lift. Don said, "No way," and I didn't have a license in NZ, but was prepared to give it a go. So off we went to Herat.

There was little traffic on the road, and mostly a desert landscape all around. There was no problem until, after about 100 km, a goat—commonly called a Judas goat—led a herd of sheep, without warning, across the path the bus was taking. I ran over the goat and six sheep. It was the middle of nowhere, not a soul around or a hint of habitation anywhere, but my fellow travelers were scared. I was scared, so the bus driver took over, and Herat was where we were going to get off.

Nothing further happened that I know of. Don and I got on a bus to Kandahar and straight through to Kabul. It was tiring, but arrival in Kabul was mind-blowing. I have never seen so many men walking around carrying guns. We got a cheap hotel about a block from The Intercontinental Hotel and not far from the dried riverbed. Kabul was primitive. We needed a rest after a week of almost continual travel, and we slept for a long time.

There is nothing much to see or do in Kabul, so we took a bus up to Bamyan province to see the giant Buddha statues carved into the hillside. I hadn't seen anything as impressive as this anywhere, until Machu Picchu in Peru, but that is another story. The Taliban blew these statues up, and NZ soldiers served in this part of Afghanistan. It was easily the loveliest place in the country. Back to Kabul, then a bus to Jalalabad and another bound for Peshawar in Pakistan through the Khyber Pass. I was really looking forward to this and was not disappointed. Unfortunately, Don and I parted company at the border, as Don had lost his vaccination certificate, and the Pakistanis wouldn't let him in, so I traveled on alone.

The road was narrow and, in places, too narrow to meet a vehicle coming in the other direction. Fortunately, this didn't happen, but we were at times perilously close to the edge and a long drop to the canyon below. I was now en route to India, but it was a turbulent time, with India and Pakistan on the verge of war over Bangladesh. One night in Peshawar, then a bus to Islamabad, and another to the border with India. Everywhere, there was evidence of a military buildup, and I hoped nothing would start until I crossed over. The Indian border was friendly, and I met other travelers who were going in my direction, so I joined them.

India had been the target when I left England, and I had got there, and believe me, the shock was enormous. I had an illusion of India as a place of peace and love, à la The Beatles, the Maharishi, Mahatma Gandhi, et al., but what I got was the biggest rat race you could ever imagine. The first train ride 3rd class to Delhi was a nightmare, but I was traveling cheap and this was the way to go. The train was packed, although we did get a seat, and our packs were all on the floor. Buying the ticket was a major hassle. There was a queue of sorts but really you had to fight your way to the ticket box, stick your hand through the grill and bellow your requirements, then you had to fight your way onto the train. The train was slow and made many stops when more people crammed ontothe train and onto the roof of the train. How could people live like this? I dozed through the journeywhen I could. Fortunately, I had some bread and water for sustenance, but it was claustrophobic.

Getting to Old Delhi station was a relief, and there were cows on the platform going about their business without a care in the world. The travelers somehow managed to stay together, and without much effort, we found a cheap hotel with a room for six beds and a fan on the ceiling, which never stopped, thank heaven. It had a cold water shower and a window that looked out onto a crowded street. It cost

10 rupees a night, which was about one USD by the official bank rate, but India was the place of the black market, and you could nearly double your money by changing with the multitude of legitimate and illegitimate money changers. But it could be hazardous; cheats and fraudsters were everywhere, as were thieves and pickpockets. Every time you went outside, you ran the gauntlet, so you had to be ruthless with your contacts and watchful every second of the day. There was no peace in an Indian city.

Once settled in the hotel room, I went out to change money and was told to go to a shop that sold precious stones, especially rubies. I went in and got the hard sell but bought nothing. I said, "I am a poor traveler," and they laughed. Compared to what was outside in the street, I was a rich man. I changed 10 pounds British, which was about 20 rupees officially, and I got 30 per pound. This could last a while, with my hotel costing 10 rupees a night.

Eating was a hazard anywhere because of the chances of getting the Delhi belly. Whenever you sat down at any eating establishment, they put a glass of water down for you, but the wise people never drank it. I always ordered a Coke, and it had to be opened in front of me, or else I wouldn't have it. Coke saved my life in India. I always ordered rice and dahl because that was the mildest curry, and I would supplement it with vegetables that I bought in the market. I also drank a lot of tea because it was served piping hot in a clay cup that you could throw away after use. I loved the way they poured it from the steaming cauldron into your cup; there was an art to it. I always had a rice cookie with it, and this diet lasted me all the way through India.

Beggars were the other hassle—"Bakshish Sahib" was the cry everywhere, which you learned to ignore. It was endless, however, so one learned to walk quickly and confidently. Beggars could not beg anywhere except their designated territory, which they paid for by some big chief. Once that territory was passed, another collection of beggars picked you up. You couldn't leave the hotel after dark because people would settle down for the night outside. Thousands slept in the street and had their own area, which they paid for as well. It was a cruel world out there, but for us travelers, we settled in our hotel room, smoking ganga through a chillum and talking shite. My hotel room was great, and I befriended an American guy called Randy, who played guitar very well. We all sang songs into the evening, stoned out of our minds but mindful of the world outside our four walls.

Tragedy did happen, and when it happens, it cuts you like a knife. A Canadian guy, who I never met but people said was deeply unhappy, jumped from the fourth floor of our hotel and died on the road outside. His body lay there for a couple of hours, and police came and asked questions. Fortunately, I was out during the day, wandering around Delhi, and saw none of it, but the hotel room buzzed with it when I got back. I decided it was time to go, as I had seen the Red Fort and walked everywhere, and I wanted to see the Taj Mahal and continue moving.

Another disturbing incident I experienced in India was when a guy I met at the Delhi hotel became very sick with what we assumed was hepatitis. He was American, and from what I gathered, he was fairly well-to-do. He was extremely unwell, so we took him to a hospital, but he was refused entry. A doctor recommended that we take him to a private hospital and provided us with an address. So we did.

We had to walk there with him hanging on to me and another guy. It was a very arduous journey, but we made it. Upon arrival, they said he could be admitted, but they demanded $25 US in cash before accepting him. We didn't have it, but the guy had a Nikon camera, which he handed over in lieu of payment. We left him there, and I never saw him again. I hope he survived. Humanity is expensive in this country.

Unfortunately, I had to stay. An old Indian stopped me in the street and told me he would tell me my fortune. I was still slightly stoned and not quite with it, but interested just the same. He asked me if I had a girlfriend, to which I replied that I didn't, but I said yes anyway. He told me to write her name on a piece of paper, which he gave me, but he could not see what I wrote. He told me to put the paper in my pocket, which I did, and he then told me her name was Jane because that was the name I had written. He then asked me for the paperback, and I gave it to him. He showed me that the name was no longer written on it. I was astonished. I gave him some change and went to walk away when I was interrupted by a well-dressed young man who said, "Welcome to India," and invited me for a cold drink in the nearby tea shop. I should never have gone. He sweet-talked me and said he could change my British pounds at 36 per pound. My eyes lit up because I could travel further. He asked me to show him what travelers' cheques I was carrying, and I did. Then I got a smack in the head from someone behind me, and the cheques were gone.

After calling myself all the silly buggers in the world and feeling sorry for myself, I went to the police, made a statement, then went to Barclays Bank, gave them the statement, and asked for replacement cheques. Fortunately, I had written all the cheque numbers in my travel book, and the bank said they would replace them, but it would take two weeks. I had other money in my money belt and could last two weeks with no problem, but the episode badly shook me, and I wanted out of Delhi quickly. I caught the train the next day for Agra and the Taj Mahal.

If there is one thing you must do in India, apart from seeing what overpopulation brings, then seeing the Taj Mahal is it. The third-class train to Agra Cant station was an ordeal, and then to see two dogs knotted on the way out made it a memorable day. The Taj Mahal was everything they say about it—magnificent—but if you go behind it, where the river flat is, and look back, then the shrine is put in its perspective. I recall later in life seeing a photograph of Princess Diana sitting on a seat where I had sat in front of the Taj Mahal, and I could say I sat where she did. At the time, as I mentioned earlier, India and Pakistan were on the verge of war over Bangladesh, and out the back, the Indian Army was getting ready to protect the Taj should an air attack come. That night, the moon shone off the dome of the Taj Mahal, and it was an awesome experience.

The next day, I took the train to Banaras (or Varanasi, as it is now called), the place where they burn the bodies. Many people come to Banaras to die, and the place was filled with pilgrims and people who lived off them, including thieves and con men. I saw a bearded man here who had no legs and one withered arm, who sat in a trolley and pushed himself around begging. I had to give him something, but once I had, I was circled by other beggars wanting the same. You can't give to everybody, as heartless as it seems. By the Hindu religion, Banaras is the place of the Gods, and on the banks of the mighty Ganges River, bodies are burnt here, and the ashes thrown in the river. Heavens, the river is dirty enough, but the people believe it is clean and pure, and that's OK by me—but I wouldn't wash in it as hundreds of people do every day.

Photography is forbidden, and I can understand that, but I did manage to take a secret shot of a funeral pyre burning. I had watched the body being put on the pyre, the wood doused in butter fat, then lit. The fire spread quickly, and people mourned. It was a moving moment, and I felt guilty taking the photograph. I walked back through the dark, narrow alleys to the main street, heading to my hotel, which was, once again, a six-bed affair shared with other hippies. It was here that one of them, an American girl whose name eludes me, gave me a copy of the *Bhagavad Gita*, a sort of Hindu Bible. The talk in the room was very spiritual, with incense burning and the chillums doing their work. I needed it, really, after being robbed in Delhi. That night, I decided I was going to Kathmandu, the capital of the mountainous country of Nepal. I would take a third-class train to Patna, then a bus to this mysterious city that I couldn't imagine.

The train was not so bad. I sat with some other hippies and started to read the *Bhagavad Gita*, which is really a long poem. I guess you have to be in the mood to read it, and preferably be in India, to take in its power and meaning. From Patna, you could see the Himalayas in all their glory, with Everest triumphant in its majesty. I looked forward to the bus ride the next day.

I underestimated the change in temperature because of the height and, unfortunately, developed a chill around my kidneys, which gave me some pain. But luck came my way in the form of a young Jewish couple who were honeymooning in India and traveling on the same bus as me. The woman was carrying antibiotics and other medication, and when she heard of my plight, she gave me some to take. They worked, and by the time the bus had climbed to over 19,000 feet—7,000 feet higher than New Zealand's highest mountain, Mt. Cook/Aorangi—I was ready for the challenges a place like Kathmandu had to offer.

The weather was cool, and I could wear jeans, a shirt, a jersey, socks, and shoes. I had missed them. I walked through the city and took in the Monkey Temple, which was hazardous if you were carrying food or anything else. The monkeys were very sharp. I stayed in a hostel with bunk accommodation and ate next door at the Snowman Cafe. Sir Ed Hillary had signed a photo on the wall of the Snowman, and the restaurant served a delicious buffalo noodle soup, which I ate every day. It also discreetly sold opium tea, which was tea with opium in it.

My first cup blew my mind, and I struggled to get back to my bunk and lie down. All was peaceful and groovy until I tried to move, then the world turned, and I became disoriented. The young lad who ran the show was brilliant, and he loved the Rolling Stones but didn't always get the lyrics right. If something on the menu wasn't available, he would sing, "You can't always get what you want." When you are stoned, that is very funny.

In my haze, an Englishman at the hostel convinced me to go trekking. I tried, but I didn't have the right boots. After a very long walk and a night outside, I called it quits and went back to Kathmandu. One more night at the Snowman, then I caught a bus back to Patna and a train to Calcutta, now called Kolkata. But before I left, I bought a khukuri knife from a young girl in the market for about $3, and I still have it. It's a Gurkha knife and an impressive blade it is.

Calcutta was a nightmare. I have never seen so many people. You couldn't move without touching someone on the streets. The hotel was twice the price of Delhi, so I had a look at the Ganges as it headed for the delta and caught the third-class train back to Delhi. I had to change trains at Varanasi for some reason and spent a night at the station. Amazingly, I met someone from Christchurch. He was the son of the editor of the *Star Sun* newspaper, but I've forgotten his name. We shared a seat for the night, and my train left in the morning.

Back in Delhi, I went straight to the bank and got my traveler's cheques with no problem, checked into my old hotel, and caught my breath. Money was short, and I needed to move further east and closer to home. In discussions in the room at night, I heard that there was a ship from Madras (now Chennai) to Penang in Malaysia, so I booked a third-class train ticket, and away I went. The only thing of note that happened on the train was that, as I slept, someone somehow stole a film canister from the bag I used to hang around my neck. It was the only thing that was missing, and ironically, it was the canister with the film I took illegally of the bodies burning at Banaras.

Was it karma?

At Madras, I checked into the YMCA and needed to stay four days before the boat sailed. England was playing India at cricket in Madras, so I went to see the match and was harangued all day by the spectators because one of the English bowlers allegedly used the Vaseline off his brow to rub on the ball. Ball tampering was not just an Aussie trick; the Poms did it first.

I had a couple of worries in Madras: the first was my dwindling money, and the second was two ulcers that had festered on my right leg and were infected. I struggled through for two days, living as cheaply as possible, then caught the boat and immediately checked in with the ship's doctor, who sorted me out with penicillin. The two-day voyage was a dream, and I ate every chance I got.

Unfortunately, I washed all my clothes on the boat and hung them out to dry on a line outside my cabin, but somebody nicked my Levis, and I was down to the ones I wore. It was life on the edge. Arriving at Penang was a different world, but I was reminded of the one I had just left, as a Pakistani gunboat was in the harbour, and I sensed that war was not far away.

I hitchhiked to KL, and it was a small city in those days. No Petronas Towers or other tall buildings. There was nothing happening, so I continued down to Port Dickson on the coast and settled into the youth hostel. It was idyllic, and the only memory I have is being caught out at sea with a water snake between me and the beach. I didn't see its beady little eyes, but I sensed that it knew where I was and was checking me out. It caused my heart to flutter. I had heard that they were very poisonous, and it seemed a long time before I got back to shore, but it was probably not more than 10 minutes.

Singapore was the next port of call, and I had heard that they were particularly hard on long hairs like myself and had refused entry to many. I hoped it wouldn't be me, as I was dreadfully short of money and had written to my brother John, asking him to send me some money to Singapore, which I would repay because I planned to travel by ship to Fremantle, Australia, where he lived.

I hitched to Johor Bahru, cleaned myself and my clothes up, and the next morning, about 7:00 a.m., I combed back my hair, gelled it down, and put it in a ponytail, got my best clothes on, carried a map of Singapore, and fronted the border. No problems at all. I bussed into the city and straight to the bank to collect my money, then to the travel agent and booked the ship, which left in a week. Then, I found a hostel with bunk accommodation and checked in.

There were other travelers, and we clicked immediately and had a great week walking around the city and at night strolling through Bugis Street, where the creatures hung out. Bugis Street has gone now, but in my day, it was world famous.

The stunning thing about Singapore then, because it wasn't the massive city it is now, was the harbour. Looking out at night, you could see more than 150 ships waiting to berth or going about their business. I took in Raffles Hotel and had tea and scones at great cost.

I had a problem to solve before I went because I had been carrying a palm-sized block of Nepalese hash and dreaded confronting Australian customs with it tucked in my underpants. I had carried it from Nepal with no problem, but now it was a crisis. My solution was this: I bought a pair of Levi jeans, which I needed, and wrapped the hash in two layers of plastic, lavishly coated with Old Spice aftershave. I put the packet in the jeans pocket, rolled it tightly, and posted it to Alan Shepherd, care of me at my Australian address. If you don't know who Alan Shepherd is, he was the first American in space. Hopefully, problem solved.

The ship journey was great, and once again, I ate every chance I got. I arrived in Fremantle with my brother waiting for me during the Christmas/New Year holiday. I needed a job quickly, and fortune favoured me. My brother worked for a marine engineering factory on the waterfront, and I went there to seek out a job on the first day of work after the holidays. There was a ship's captain waiting in the office, and he asked me if I was looking for a job, and he hired me on the spot. The job was to take the rust off the hull of a boat called the Kuri Pearl, which was in a dry dock in the factory grounds. With two other guys, we chipped, sanded, and painted the hull of the Kuri Pearl until it was fit to sail. The lads and I were asked if we would like to crew the ship on a voyage up the West Australian coast to Broome and then be delivered back with another ship returning to Fremantle. "Yes" was our response, and who wouldn't?

I paid my brother back with my first pay, moved into a boarding house, and on the same day, my jeans turned up from Singapore. I was over the moon. The journey up the West Coast was quite rough, and I had wisely bought seasick pills as the boat was small and was tossed around like a cork. I had also had another piece of good fortune. The Indonesian cook got appendicitis, and us lads were asked if we could cook. I said yes, and the job was mine, with more pay than a deckhand. So I cooked for the captain and crew, which was us, plus a first mate who was an angry bastard, and I had my own cabin. The lads slept in the prow of the ship. I got stoned looking out over the sea, and I was in heaven.

Broome was a sight. The tide there was massive, and when it came in and out, it had some power. The Kuri Pearl belonged to Micki Moto Pearls, and on board were two giant tanks filled with seawater. Divers in full diving kit operated off the decks, taking oysters off the bottom and settling them in the tanks for shipment around to Kuri Bay, where scientists used them to make pearls by inserting grains inside the oyster. I could have stayed and done that, but I was yearning for home, so I sailed back to Fremantle with the other ship.

On arrival back, I had to go to the shipping office in Perth to collect my pay, and it was enough to get me to Sydney and a flight to New Zealand. I decided to try and hitchhike and got to Kalgoorlie before the cops saw me, checked me over, and made me catch a bus. Fair enough, I thought—I wasn't going to argue with a block of hash in my pack.

Got to Sydney, bought an airline ticket to Auckland, and this was to be my first major flight, and another amazing thing happened. I had little money left, so decided to walk to the airport from downtown Sydney and stay the night at the airport while awaiting my flight. On the way out, an Aussie soldier who was on leave from Vietnam stopped me, and we had a friendly chat. He flagged down a taxi, gave the driver $20, and told him to take me to the airport. I was stunned. Lady luck had been on my side—long may it last.

From Auckland, I hitched to Wellington, crossed over to Picton by ferry, and hitched to Christchurch, arriving in the Square around midnight. I walked home, the door was unlocked, left my pack in the kitchen, and bedded down. In the morning, my father, on his way to work, opened the door and said, "Oh, you're back."

Being back in Christchurch and living at home was strange for me. My mother was brilliant, but she did say that I had got hard. I agreed but told her I had to. It was clear my younger brothers didn't want me there, so I moved out into a flat on the corner of Salisbury and Madras streets with Terry Austin and his girlfriend, Marie. Terry was about to go on holiday to his home country, England, and the rent suited me. I had gotten a job at Marlin Carpets as a storeman, thanks to my father, and I started saving to travel again. I knew I couldn't stop—there was so much of the world yet to see.

My friend Dave May, who we called Harry Mouldy, talked of a ship leaving for South America from Wellington, and the idea appealed, but I had little money. Because I had worked only half a year in England, I applied for a tax rebate, and this boosted my savings, allowing me to buy a ticket to Argentina, along with Harry, with the ship leaving in late November 1972. The voyage was brilliant as we sailed south and west through the Straits of Magellan and up the east coast of South America to Buenos Aires. The good air.

The ship was the Angelina Lauro, which was later to be hijacked by terrorists in the Mediterranean. Remarkably, on board was a fellow traveler whom I had met on my journey overland. His name was Bekir, and he stood out because he had been in Turkey and converted to Islam. To show he was serious, he got circumcised and was in great pain when I met him. I could not understand why anyone would voluntarily do that, but in my experience, humans will always surprise you. He did do another thing that I helped him out with. At the passengers' concert, he did a version of Rolf Harris's *Jake the Peg*. I helped with the lyrics, and it was a bloody good laugh.

Going through the Straits of Magellan was magical. The history of the place was haunting and wrecked ships still lay where they fell. It was freezing cold, with Tierra del Fuego flat and barren, with oil field flares lighting the way at times. Harry and I disembarked at Buenos Aires on December 2, 1972, along with an Argentine national, Nick Warr, who was a fabulous man and whom we were to stay with before starting on our journey through the continent of South America.

Digging manholes in Sydney 1969 with Jimmy Docherty who thought we were related.

Graduation with B.A 1969. I used it only once to get a job.

Johnny Parsons and I getting pissed in Tahiti. Southern Cross ship in background.

Xmas Day 1970 at the Forest gate Pub with the Aussie boys and Parsons

The Ford boys at Blackpool 1971. We slept in the back of a van. Ian in front was a good mate.

Fountain de Trevi Rome 1971. Me looking for coins and there were plenty. I did go back in 2007.

On the beach at Corfu with Melanie a good friend.

Singing an Elvis song at the Acropolis Athens 1971. Got a round of applause from tourists.

Walking through the ruins of Ephesus Turkey. It was stunning.

Ferry across the Bosphorus. Europe into Asia. They have a bridge
over the Bosphorus now.

The bus broke down in Turkey. My Canadian mate Don Faucett, we traveled through to Pakistan.

About to get moved along outside the Shah's palace in Teheran.

The bus I drove in Afghanistan with fateful consequences for a goat and 6 sheep.

Arrival in Kathmandu with randy and John after an horrific drive up the Himalayas from India.

SOUTH AMERICA
(December 1972 – 3 May 1973)

When I first contemplated South America, the things I most wanted to do were to see Rio de Janeiro, visit Machu Picchu, and go down the Amazon. But there was so much more to South America than I could ever have imagined.

I was planning to travel on the cheap again and calculated that I could spend about $3.00 a day, so things were tight. I was going to have to spend a fair bit of time sleeping under the stars, which is always fraught with danger. I was also aware that I would need to learn some Spanish phrases and words that travelers use all the time—such as "What time is it?", "Do you have hot showers?", the days of the week, counting, and "How much?" etc. I got a Spanish/English dictionary and kept a book where I wrote down useful things to say. I enjoyed this, and by the time I got to Mexico, I could conduct a reasonable conversation, but it's all gone now.

There is not much to see in Argentina, but they do play football, and as a keen aficionado of the game, I went to La Boca to see Boca Juniors play Independiente in Buenos Aires. La Boca was a scary place, and I got out fast after the game. The game finished 0-0, so I didn't get to see the celebrations that go with a goal being scored in this part of the world.

Downtown Buenos Aires is spacious, and I wandered along Florida, the great shopping area, and even saw a couple of tango dancers. There was obvious poverty, and the country had been through political turmoil, with the hangover from that still evident. Nick, when he got back, had to report to the police station, and when he went to do so, he said, "I might not be back." He wasn't.

On further reflection, you would think that Argentina should have been a prosperous country, but it's not. Inflation was out of control, and no commodity was the same price two days in a row; it was always going up. Out in the countryside, buildings and towns had a rundown appearance. The whole situation bemused me.

Harry and I took to the road, hitchhiking around and having some magic moments. Halfway to Salta in the North, we passed a road-working gang who called out to us as we waited at the side of the road. We chatted away and told them we had come from New Zealand, and we were floored by a chorus of "All Blacks!" They were in awe. We waited for a long time, and it started to rain. Harry and I used to sing old songs as we waited, and as we finished "Me and My Shadow," it started to bucket down, so we made our way back to the road gang and asked if we could bed down with them in their hut. We were welcomed, and they shared their meal with us. It was a heartwarming night.

We got to the lovely town of Salta, then went south along the world's longest straight road to a place called Bahia Blanca. We had a meal of Milanesa, then went to see a Woody Allen film called "Bananas," and rolled with laughter to the surprise of the rest of the audience. We walked out of Bahia Blanca afterward and slept on the beach, then continued on to Mar del Plata the next day.

Harry and I split then, and he went back to Nick's place in Buenos Aires for Christmas. After a couple of days on the beach, I joined them. Christmas was spent waterskiing on the Paraná River, and when we were joined at Nick's place by a couple of other passengers from the Angelino Lauro, we decided to go to Uruguay.

We checked out Punta del Este, which was to grow hugely as a port for the Round the World Yacht Race, but when we were there, it was a small holiday resort with a shipwrecked vessel on the beach. We played football on the beach and looked out to sea, where the German battleship Graf Spee was scuttled during World War II.

On to Montevideo, and for the first time, I felt that we were in South America. There was a salsa-like feeling and energy about the place. We arrived in the middle of a demonstration where fists punched the air and chanting told their story of woe. We wanted to get away, as you don't want to attract the eye of the authorities in this part of the world; it tends to cost you money. On the way out, we met a man yelling "helados, helados," he was selling ice cream, and that brought a smile to our faces.

I wanted to stay on the East coast and make my way to Brazil and Rio de Janeiro, but the feeling of the group was to go back west to Argentina and up to Paraguay, so we did. However, it instilled in me a need to get out on my own, and shortly, that would come without rancor, I am happy to say.

Paraguay was very hot, with temperatures in the 40s, and was remarkable immediately because of the number of women in charge of businesses and selling things. I found out that because of wars with their neighbors, Paraguay had more women than men, but it was ruled by a dictator called Stroessner, whose name was written everywhere in Asunción, the capital.

Harry and I were alone now, and we decided to go upriver to a place called Concepción, where a Nazi war criminal, Josef Mengele, lived. He was later caught in Argentina, but seeing his house was eerie. It was a lively trip, but Harry and I decided to part ways. He went north to Bolivia, and I went back east to see Brazil and Rio.

I stayed in Asunción for one night and met a Swiss guy called Marcel, who had a NZ girlfriend and whom he missed big time. He was going to Bolivia, but we were to meet again in Peru a couple of weeks later and ended up going all the way to the USA, where we were parted on the road to Los Angeles and never met again.

The next day, I took a bus to the Iguazú Falls, the most spectacular falls I have ever seen, which formed the border between Argentina,

Paraguay, and Brazil. I then walked back to the border, and the Paraguay guard ran down the road towards me, shaking his head and telling me to go away. I bellowed at him, "Salida, salida!" which means "I am leaving," and he cooled down, stamped my passport, and I walked over the Friendship Bridge into Brazil. That night, I was robbed of my camera and a shirt, but I yelled and screamed, and the four guys fucked off quickly. I was lucky, so I got on a bus straight to Rio, and my luck changed big time.

I got to Rio late afternoon the next day, and the view was magnificent. Pão de Açúcar (Sugarloaf) and Corcovado stood out on the hills around Rio, and to my left, I could see the road to Ipanema beach. I walked to the youth hostel, but it was closed, and then, the first stroke of luck. I was approached by an Australian guy called Jack, who had rented an apartment across the harbor from Rio in a place called Niterói and needed people to help pay the rent. It was on the tenth floor, and the lift didn't work, and water ran at a trickle, but never mind. Two Canadian girls and a Coloured South African also stayed, so we had a party ready to go.

The view of Rio at night was stunning as we watched the city light up and aircraft land at the airport. We spent our days at the beach, both at Niterói and over at Flamengo and Botafogo, and wandered the city, which had its fair share of beggars and roughnecks. Care was needed with every move.

Football called, and Jack and I went to Maracanã Stadium, which holds over 100,000 people, and saw a local derby between Botafogo, who played in black and white, and Fluminense, who played in red and white. It was 2-2, and the crowd went nuts when a goal was scored. Rio was fabulous, but I couldn't stay; it was too expensive.

From what I had experienced so far, I didn't dare hitchhike, so I decided to take a train the next morning to Baru, and then another across Brazil to Corumbá on the Bolivian border. That night, we all got pissed and stoned on some form of jungle juice, and I missed the train because I slept in.

What luck!! The train I was supposed to be on derailed outside São Paulo, and there were casualties. This was to happen to me again later on my journey, but I was shocked.

I took a bus to São Paulo with the intention of taking the train to Baru, then on to Corumbá, and I did so without major incident.

São Paulo was a massive city, very busy, but I made my way to the railway station and caught the train to Baru. It was a lovely town with gardens in the center, and as I had four hours until the train to Corumbá, I sat in the gardens and contemplated my plight. Getting robbed had affected me greatly, and I was determined it should never happen again. I put it down to being too trusting, to having developed an easy-going hippy personality, and decided it had to go. While in London, I had admired the Cockney manner and accent; it was knowing, witty, and aggressive, and my mate Harry had a Cockney accent that I could imitate at will. So that is what I did. I became a Cockney.

An extraordinary and quite disturbing thing happened while I was sitting in the gardens at Baru. Two young girls, possibly not much older than 12 years, offered me sexual favors for little money, and they wouldn't go away. I had to get up and leave, and amazingly, it was not the last time that this happened. It was also to happen on a train in Colombia. What is it about trains?

The train to Corumbá was a two-day journey, so I settled in for the ride as we crossed the Mato Grosso and started reading a book I picked up in Rio called Passions of the Mind about Sigmund Freud. It was brilliant. I also met a couple of American Peace Corps workers who spoke fluent Portuguese and were making their way back to America. Their relationship was often antagonistic, and their fights were hilarious, but they were both good company, and I was glad to test my new personality on them.

My aim was now Machu Picchu, and I wanted to get there quickly while seeing La Paz and Lake Titicaca. We got through the Bolivian border and went to Santa Cruz, immediately to Cochabamba, then took a bus over the mountains to La Paz. You could feel the altitude at La Paz immediately, and I had much to do here, as I had had mail sent to American Express in La Paz and had been told that if I wanted an American Visa, then the US Embassy in La Paz was the best place to get one.

We found a cheap hotel with no agua caliente (hot water) and set about doing business. I applied immediately for a visa at the US Embassy and requested a transit visa, as I planned to fly to Miami, see New Orleans and New York, then fly to London. I was neatly dressed and provided evidence of money, and two days later, I had a 3-month transit visa to the USA stamped in my passport, and there was hope ahead.

Walking around La Paz was quite exhausting and cool. The walls were all marked with Viva Banzer, the current dictator in Bolivia. I saw streets with coca leaf bales stacked 3 and 4 high, ready for processing into cocaine. Many locals, especially the local Indians, chewed coca leaves with a substance called lime to bring out the energy. I decided to use it too, and it certainly helped, but it loosened a filling at the back of one of my front teeth, and it needed dentist work.

I found a dentist, a husband-and-wife affair. The husband did the drilling while the wife pedaled the drill. At first, the dentist kept asking me if I had pain (dolor). I said no, as he wanted to pull my tooth out. I insisted on a filling, and he did so without anesthesia. The wife pedaled like blazes, and I can assure you I was glad when it was finished. It cost me about $3 US, and remarkably, I still have that filling today. All during the ordeal, the wife kept asking me if I liked

Tom Jones. She put the EEE accent at the end, and I would nod from time to time, and she put a Tom Jones record on. It's Not Unusual, I thought.

The next day, I went to American Express, as I carried their travelers' cheques, and collected my mail, but the city was quiet, and there were tanks outside major buildings, and troops were everywhere. I wanted no trouble, so I scuttled back to my hotel and read my book. I was reading about the Sigmund Freud Rat Man case, and it was fascinating. The tanks in the street had worried me and my companions, and we were scared that the borders would be closed, so we headed for Copacabana, near Lake Titicaca and the border of Peru, and crossed over.

Peru had the Sol as its currency, and you could buy them at a superior rate to that in Peru in Bolivia, so I loaded up before crossing, and we headed north to Puno, a large town on Lake Titicaca. No buses were running, so we somehow got a truck and headed north and found the road flooded. The truck eased its way across the flooded roads while I and the American couple sat on bales in the back of the truck. It was slow progress, and it started to rain, and I was glad of my poncho groundsheet, which covered my head and backpack.

Five hours of this took us to Puno, and the floodwaters covered many streets there. Luck smiled on me again, and a Catholic priest from the church on high ground in the town invited us to stay in the church. We accepted, of course, but I felt it was a bit grim that the locals were not invited to do the same—it was their town, after all. The next day was fine, and we caught a bus to Cusco in deepest, darkest Peru, and on the hills that surrounded this magnificent city were the words "Viva El Perú" carved into the hillside. Machu Picchu was in range.

The week I spent in Cusco was probably one of the best weeks I have ever had in my life. Cusco was a small place, and I got a pension about a block behind Plaza de Armas. The market was not far away, and the food was good and cheap. For the first time, it felt like I was back on the road in Asia; the camaraderie was the same. I shared the room with an American couple and a couple of others, and we got on famously. My Cockney persona was a winner, particularly with the Americans, and they couldn't do enough for me.

On the first night, they bought a gram of cocaine, and we snorted it through a tube with a bowl at the end. It was pure and uncut, and the feeling was brilliant. We decided to go to the movies, as Cabaret was playing just out of town. We walked there, and I just felt like I was in heaven. I wasn't hungry, and I had energy to burn. No wonder they called it Peruvian marching powder. I knew nothing about Cabaret, but afterwards became a firm fan of Liza Minnelli. I barely slept, got up, and walked to Saksaywaman, an old Inca fortress with the walls all slotted together perfectly without cement. In fact, I walked around the whole town, I was still up there.

Machu Picchu beckoned, and early in the morning, a few of us went to the station for a steam train journey to Aguas Calientes, the station at the bottom of the hill from Machu Picchu. Before writing this episode, I read that in 2023, more than a million people visited Machu Picchu, and here was I, going to see this magnificent historical Inca ruin in 1973 with half a dozen people. On the two days that I spent there, less than 50 people visited the ruins.

On getting off the train, there was a low mist over everything. Looking up, so nothing could be seen. A road wound up the hill to the hotel at the top, but everyone on the train headed for a track that led upwards, so I joined them. I had bought an Inca woolen hat made of llama hair, which I still have, as it was quite cool, and made my way up the slippery slope. It took about 25 minutes and came out at the white building of the international hotel. Machu Picchu was off to the right, but you could see very little, and dusk was upon us.

Some of the travelers asked at the hotel if we could sleep on the veranda, but they said no, so where to sleep became a problem. There was a ticket box that about 6 people could squeeze into, so I staked my claim and parked my pack where I intended to sleep. At altitude, you get tired very quickly, and after a feed of bread and cheese from my pack reserves, I managed to doze off.

The morning broke fine and clear about 6:00 am, and I stared out through the ticket box, and there it was—Machu Picchu, with Huayna Picchu looking down proudly from on high. I was in awe, but the ticket box didn't open until 9:00 am, so we speculated about what made the Incas build such a magnificent home in such an isolated place? They must have been desperate and scared. We were first through the gate at 9:00 am and roamed the stone houses and grassy levels. I, and two others, decided to climb Huayna Picchu, and it proved remarkably easy, although it looked very difficult. We were aided by a low wire close to the ground that you could hold onto because it was steep. At the top, it was magnificent, and you could look down on the raging Urubamba River as it circled around. I can still see it in my mind's eye today.

The train back to Cusco left mid-afternoon, so we wandered back down the slope and found a place to eat before the slow journey back. My thoughts were agog at what I had seen. Few places on this planet could compare to Machu Picchu. It's a must-see.

No trip to South America would be complete without an encounter with a llama, and I had mine in the market at Cusco. There was an enclosure at the market where llamas were traded, and I went to have a look. I love the face of a llama; it is inquisitive, humorous, with a hint of mischief, and I wanted to look one in the eye. So I did. They have long eyelashes, and you can see personality there. I bent down, got as close as I could. It looked at me curiously, then spat chewed-up grass in my face. Everyone fell about laughing while I wiped green drool from my face. I thanked the llama, saluted it, and walked away green-faced. You just have to do it.

Back at Cusco, the hotel buzzed. People were up there in their minds still, but my journey had to continue. I had two routes out of Cusco, both by bus. One went through Ayacucho, but rumor had it that a Maoist rebel group called the Shining Path was in the area, so I ruled that out—and was happy I did. Some Westerners were kidnapped, as I heard about later on my journey.

The bus I took went through Abancay and on to Nazca, where the mysterious Lines of Nazca were. The road down from the Andes was high, and you could look down on the Nazca Lines and see the creatures etched into the desert landscape by the Nazca people around 200 BC.

The bus trip was nerve-wracking. When you get on a bus in Peru, there are always young boys who, for a small fee, will stack your pack in the roof rack. After all that had happened to me, I trusted no one and did this myself, always stacking my pack in the center, away from the edge, even though the luggage was tied down. Inside the bus, it was a squash. At times on the road, when the road got narrow, everybody had to get off the bus as the driver edged his way past some tricky bends where to fall meant certain death. I wasn't ready for that and willingly walked behind the bus.

Once past Nazca, the road came out on the coast all the way to Lima, and I have to admit it was great to see the sea again. Now I had to pursue my Amazon River dream.

Lima was a big city, and when I arrived early in the morning, I walked around the empty streets looking for a cheap hotel that I had been told about, eventually finding it in a plaza close to the poor side of town where a bridge led over the river. Two things happened in Lima that made life interesting and memorable. First, I met an American guy called Stan, although I don't think that was his real name. He said, after we had had a few tokes of Colombian weed, that he was wanted in America because he had dodged the draft that would have taken him to Vietnam.

It was a good story. Then he told me that Lima was famous for its cockfights: two roosters with razors on their spurs, starved and then set to fight to the death. He suggested we go look for one, but we were both well stoned and we laughed and laughed uncontrollably as we tried to ask people where a cockfight was. We knew no Spanish words for it, so we came up with "pollo combate," a fighting chicken. When asking, we would raise our fists in a boxer's stance and say "pollo combate," then we would erupt in uncontrollable laughter. We never found what we were looking for, but it was one of the funniest nights I ever had. In the morning, when I woke, I found that Stan had done a bunk without paying his bill. The owners looked at me to settle, but I told them correctly that I had only just met him and it wasn't my responsibility.

I decided to go to the beach for the day and found a bus that took me to La Herradura. It was a fabulous beach with surf, but the water was freezing. I was approached by a Peruvian girl who wanted to speak English, so I agreed. The first thing she asked me was, "Are you Católica?" Catholic. I said no; I am not into that sort of thing. We had a coffee, I told her I was from New Zealand. "Nova Zelandia!!" she exclaimed and clutched her hands to her heart. "You must come for dinner." So I did. It was a humble household, no father, but two sisters and a brother, and we had guinea pig as the main course in a stew. It was served as little bite-sized balls and, to be honest, was quite tasty. When I left, she wanted my address and telephone number, so I gave it, and she wanted to meet me the next day. I said OK but had no intention of keeping the appointment; it just seemed the easiest way out. She was likable, but I was on a mission.

The postscript to the story was I heard from my mother in a letter that the girl had phoned her and wanted to know where I was. Mum handled it in the way mothers do.

The next day I researched the way to the Amazon and booked a train to Cerro de Pasco, a bus to Tingo Maria—which was over the Andes on the altiplano—then a bus to Pucallpa on the Amazon River. The train left the next day, so that was that.

Even though the train was not comfortable, with wooden benches for seats, this train journey was also a highlight of my South America trip because it was a switchback journey to cross over the Andes. The train would go forward along a track, then backward up another line, then forward again, and so on to the top. As we went up, the air cooled, and a change into jeans, socks, and shoes was necessary. In Lima, it had been in the 80s°F and humid, and that dropped to the 50s°F, but as we progressed to Cerro de Pasco, things warmed up. I could have stayed there but decided to go on to Tingo Maria, where I rested for the night in what was the most comfortable bed I had had in South America. Unfortunately, the bus to Pucallpa left at 6:00 a.m. in the morning, so the chance of a lie-in was thwarted. The alarm clock that I had was a godsend as I would never have woken had it not jarred me awake at 5:30.

The bus to Pucallpa was more of the same. I had to fight to get my luggage on top of the bus and in the center, then squirm into a seat. The journey was not easy, as floods had covered the road, and we had to be towed through by bulldozer. When we reached Pucallpa, it was early evening. I found a cheap sleeping establishment and met a number of other travelers who were looking to go down the Amazon as well.

The Amazon was not wide at Pucallpa, but there were a number of boats of different shapes and sizes, from canoes up to barge size. The one I was to get on was actually two ferry-sized boats joined together: one side carried cargo and oil drums, the other was for passengers, the majority of whom were travelers like myself, going to Iquitos. There were many Amazon Indians to be seen, and they were quite attractive people with colorful garb. Few approached us, though; they were private and modest.

The journey was to take 3 days, mainly because of stops along the way, and the river was quite swift in parts. I saw no piranha but never considered a swim. During the daytime, I read *Dr. Zhivago*. The icy Russian winter clashed nicely with the 80-degree heat and 90% humidity, but fortunately, on the river, mosquitoes and such were not a problem. Many passengers had hammocks, which were strung out at night and taken down during the day. I slept on the deck. I loved watching the jungle go by and seeing small settlements of Indians. It was calm and peaceful.

On board was a boy, probably about 17 years old, who told us his father was a general in the Peruvian army. He was a nice enough lad and always trying to get in on what us travelers were doing. We called him *hombre pollo*, which translated to "chicken man." He seemed to like it, and it caused a few laughs. He did have plenty of money, but I wasn't convinced about his father.

Iquitos was a hassle. I stayed one night and basically ate big time, then booked a boat going the opposite direction from which we came, up the Huallaga River to Yurimaguas, deep in the jungle. It was against the current and a lot slower, but the river narrowed considerably, and we could see more of the Amazon life. Yurimaguas had been an old mission station, and on the walls of the room in which we slept were photographs of the wild Indians and a story about a slaughter that occurred there.

The mission house did serve good meals, and it was peaceful. I had chosen Yurimaguas because it had an airport, and planes flew over the Andes to Chiclayo on the Peruvian coast. Before going on the small plane, which was booked first-come, first-served, everything was weighed, and once the weight limit was reached, no more. Just as well the plane flew low over the Andes, and it shook most of the time. By the time we landed at Chiclayo, I was a nervous wreck. It was here that I met Marcel again, the Swiss I had first met weeks ago in Asuncion, Paraguay. He was heading north like me and was aiming for the USA. We decided to travel together and were not parted until hitching on the road to Los Angeles months later. Ecuador was the next country.

I am afraid to say I saw little of Ecuador. My money was running out, and I wanted to get to America. I did go to an amazing market at a place called Banos, where all the Indian women wore hats, and the origin of the Panama hat was to be found. It was a peaceful place. On to Quito and to Mitad del Mundo, or as we know it, the equator. There was a monument on the equator with a line going down the middle, and I had a photo taken of myself with a foot in either hemisphere.

I did consider going to Guayaquil, where a boat could be caught to the Galapagos Islands, but finances were not favorable, so it was Colombia, here we come.

All the time I was traveling north, I met travelers going in the other direction, and all of them said, "Watch yourself; it is dangerous." I heard stories of robberies in the street and rip-offs, so Marcel and I approached Colombia with a cautious, wary frame of mind. We knew that there was a cocaine war going on between Cali and Medellín and vowed to stay away from any of that, but we did cherish Colombian weed, which, in my opinion, is the best in the world.

We bused straight to Cali, found a hotel, and scored some weed off the manager. We then learned from travelers that Popayan was the place to go. Apparently, magic mushrooms grew in the fields around Popayan, and there was a pre-Columbian historical site called Alto de los Ídolos not far away. With my interest in ancient civilizations, Popayan had its appeal, so we went there next.

We had a problem with weed because we didn't have a pipe. Finding zigzag cigarette papers proved impossible all over South America, so

I used the thin pages of my Spanish/English dictionary, and that solved the problem. Colombian weed was very strong; you just needed a couple of tokes, and you were there. After we had a joint in Cali, we went out to eat and couldn't find our way back to the hotel. We retraced our steps back to the restaurant and realized we had walked the wrong way. We eventually got back, but a lesson was learned, and we felt fortunate that we had not run into more serious trouble. I vowed then not to smoke while traveling around the city or town or on transport and to leave it until settled in accommodation.

Popayan was brilliant. We found a brilliant place to stay where lots of travelers stayed. It was on Calle 2, but I can't remember the name. The food was great, and there was a beautiful garden. I recall watching a hummingbird feeding from an orchid-sized flower and noticing it flying backward and forward in one place, its long beak dipping into the flower. I later learned that the hummingbird is the only bird that can fly backward, and I had seen it.

With others, we decided to go looking for magic mushrooms and to take in Alto de los Ídolos at the same time. Apparently, the best place was at kilometer 14, so we got off the bus there and wandered about. The fear was of eating poisonous mushrooms, but we had been told the real magic mushrooms had a yellow glow on top and were blue underneath. We found them, but I am afraid nothing happened when I ate them at first until we reached Alto de los Ídolos. Then it was like a rush, and I sat amongst the pre-Colombian idols, tripping out of my mind. Every vow I had taken about Colombia was broken. One of the girls in our group was having a bad trip, and there is nothing worse than this when it occurs. Paranoia spreads quickly, and it did.

"Take vitamin C," everybody said, so we found a pharmacy and did, and it seemed to calm people down. It certainly did for me. Back on the bus to Popayan, I got the good feeling back, ate heartily that night, and slept like a log. "Never again," I said to myself in the morning.

I took a bus to Neiva, then a train to Bogotá. I knew we had to be fully alert in Bogotá, and when we got there, it was packs on the back and walk swiftly, like we meant it, to one of the cheap hotels that surround every railway or bus station. Something happened on the train that disturbed me, just as it had when I was in Baru, Brazil. On the train, two young girls approached me and Marcel offering sexual favors. We declined, of course, but they persisted all the way to Bogotá and tried to follow us when we disembarked. We ran for it, and being reasonably fit because of all the walking we did, we lost them and ducked into a hotel.

We stayed one night, walked around the city for half a day, then got out on a train heading north. We had heard that there was a flight from Cartagena on the Caribbean Coast to a Colombian Island called San Andrés and then on to San José, Costa Rica. That was our plan, and heading north as fast as possible was our tactic. We took a train as far north as it would go and got out to take a bus to Bucaramanga. A bus was waiting, but we were hungry and needed to refresh ourselves, so we told the driver of the bus what we were doing and asked if there was another bus later. He said there was, but after we ate, he was still there. He had waited for us. The bus ride was torturous, over roads that were very dicey and, at times, frightening, but we arrived in Bucaramanga in one piece, settled in at a hotel, and got stoned.

The next day, the paper headlines told of a bus crash on the same route we had taken the day before. Fate had smiled on me once again.

We traveled then to Barranquilla, which had a fearsome reputation, and quickly got on a bus to Cartagena along the coast. In later life, I went to see the film with Michael Douglas called *Romancing the Stone*, which was filmed partly in Cartagena, an old pirate port on the Caribbean. It was a lovely place, and I remember coming into the town and seeing a sculpture of a pair of laced shoes on a roundabout entering the city. We stayed long enough to buy a plane ticket to San José via San Andrés, and off we flew. Goodbye, South America, hello, Central America.

There was one final thing I had to do before departure. I had some wonderful Colombian weed that I didn't want to part with, but how to get through customs was a problem. I finally rolled it up in several plastic bags to about half an inch wide and poked it down the frame of my backpack, sealing the top again. Would it work? Well, I was soon to find out.

San Andrés was a dream. A beautiful island in the Caribbean with a lovely climate and white sand beaches. Marcel and I stayed two days and nights at a boarding house run by a big black woman who loved talking to Marcel with his Swiss-French accent. She cooked us two marvelous breakfasts, and when we left, she gave Marcel a big hug.

Landing in San José would be a test, and I knew it. The best trick is to walk confidently off the plane and through the immigration and customs hall, which I did. I was heading to the far end. Soldiers were stopping passengers and searching their luggage as they went, and one beckoned me over. I pointed to the exit and kept going. My pack was opened, my passport stamped, and through I went. A big risk, I knew, and I vowed never to do it again, but I did.

Central America, to me, meant two things: Mayan and Aztec ruins and culture, and I was to see plenty of these, and it was all brilliant.

CENTRAL AMERICA AND MEXICO

The most astonishing thing about Central America for the traveler is that there are six different currencies to deal with in a relatively small area – Costa Rica had the colón, Nicaragua the córdoba, Honduras the lempira, Guatemala the quetzal, and Belize the dollar. But the US$ was god as it was everywhere, and nobody turned it down. All the changing was a pain, and of course, you could only change notes. All part of the skills of traveling, which few people understand.

Costa Rica had a friendly vibe about it, which was a pleasant surprise after the tensions of Colombia. There was no army in this small country, and there was a strong religious presence, especially from American missionaries who were about to help me out. We spent a couple of pleasant days in San José, where I got reacquainted with the music of Carlos Santana. There was a music shop just down the street from our hotel, and the young guy in there played Santana all day. I got stoned and sat outside singing to *Oye Como Va*. He invited me in, and I surprised myself at how well I could conduct a conversation in Spanish. I had learned a lot.

Marcel and I decided to go back to hitchhiking after giving it up in Ecuador and Colombia, and we were successful as we made our way to the Nicaraguan border. We slept about 100 meters to the side of the Pan American Highway after first banging rocks on the ground to drive away snakes, but snakes were not going to be the problem. When I awoke, I put on my boots and socks and started packing my gear away when I felt a sharp pain in my left hand. I looked down and there was a scorpion wriggling on the ground. I panicked. After jumping up and down on the dark, purplish-colored scorpion to ensure that it was dead, I rushed out onto the highway and flagged down the first motorist. I was in luck. It was a youth missionary leader who spoke good English, and he drove me to the mission center in the town he was going to. There, I saw a medic who assured me I was in no danger but said I might feel some side effects—and he wasn't wrong.

We caught a lift to the border and crossed into Nicaragua, making our way to the lake and a small adobe pension for a meal and a sleep. The next morning, I had a very stiff neck that hurt with every move I made. We decided to keep traveling and got a lift to just outside Granada, close to the capital city of Managua, which had been destroyed by an earthquake in 1972. We could see no signs of habitation, just wrecked buildings, and most of it was fenced off, so we continued on to Honduras.

One of the things that made Marcel a very good traveling companion was that he liked to play cards, as did I, and we played thousands of games of a progressive whist game, in which on the first deal you got 10 cards and had to predict how many tricks you would get. If you won, you got the number of tricks plus 10 points. On the next deal, you got 9 cards, then 8, and so on, down to 1. The competition was fierce, and we were very even.

My sore neck made life intolerable; it took about 5 days to go away, and I was frazzled. Honduras came and went, but it was no fault of the country and its attractions. The best part of Honduras was on the Caribbean coast, and we had no intention of going there. Tegucigalpa was a ho-hum capital city. We stayed one night and tried to hitch the next day with little success. We were going to El Salvador. There was no love lost between Salvadorans and Hondurans. They once fought a war over a football match. It took us all day to get a ride, and then there was a disagreement with the driver of the truck who wanted money. We said it was autostop, which means hitchhiking, but because we were in the hills and miles from anywhere, we gave him the last of our Honduran money. Then we got lucky.

As we were standing there looking forlorn and downcast, a smart-looking ute stopped, and a smiling face looked out at us. He was the owner of a hacienda just down the road and asked if we would like to stay the night. I should say at this point that it was easy to realize we were overseas travelers because my backpack had a British Union Jack sewn onto it, and I always faced this to the oncoming traffic. We said thanks very much, and we went to his impressive house, where something unique happened gastronomically. We had iguana for supper. It was white flesh, a bit like a cross between fish and chicken, and it had a strong but palatable taste. Our host was a genial guy, and he was alone as his family was in Tegucigalpa, and he had returned to sort some business out. We slept long, and then back on the road, where we waited without luck for most of the day but started walking. It was nighttime before we saw the lights of civilization below us, but the road was winding and unlit. We walked down the middle of the road, flicking our torches from time to time, and eventually got down to the flat in a small town, which fortunately had a pension we could check into. What we didn't know at the time was that we had, in fact, crossed into El Salvador without any customs or border stop.

We caught a bus into San Salvador, and it was a bustling, vibrant city. We settled in our pension, and within an hour of checking in, there was a knock on the door of our room. It was two girls wanting to know if we wanted a bit of fun for 3 dollars American. I couldn't afford it, so I went for a walk and decided I needed to have more money. I wrote home for help. I had an insurance policy that I wanted canceled, which would give a small rebate. I didn't need money urgently, but I wanted to have proof of money in a bank in Los Angeles to help with entry into the USA, which was now imperative.

The next day, we took a bus to Guatemala.

Guatemala City was impressive, with the new buildings having Mayan art and cultural symbols built into them. We had learned from travelers that a good, cheap hotel was at the corner of Avenida 13 and Calle 13, and there was one. It also had a restaurant attached, and we could feed on my favorite meal of rice and beans with fried potatoes and bananas. We had also learned that the Mayan ruins at Tikal, in the northwest of the country, were impressive, and that became our goal. But first, we heard of a volcano that was easy to climb, called Chicabal, which was near a town with the fantastic name of Quetzaltenango. There was also another town nearby called Chichicastenango. I loved saying that name, and we just had to go there, so we did. It was a winding, tortuous road through forest, but we got to Chichicastenango in the morning, looked around the market, ate there cheaply, then got on another bus for Quetzaltenango. We found a pension, which was full of travelers, and researched a trip to climb Chicabal.

It was an early morning bus to the lakeside, across the lake in a small boat, then the climb. At first, it was easy through the tropical forest. Then we came out into the open and faced a few hundred meters of scree and sharp stones that cut at your shoes and hands when you had to steady yourself. The view from the top was spectacular, and we could see the highest peak in Central America, Tajumulco, also a volcano. Getting down was fun, skidding down the volcanic ash and running through the jungle to Lake Atitlán. It was brilliant, but it wrecked my boots, which were going anyway.

Back at the pension, everybody was in a fun mood, and the weed came out. The next day, we were off back to Guatemala City and a trip to Flores, the gateway town to Tikal. Before we left, I visited the market because I had noted a guy with a sewing machine contraption that could sew up boots and shoes, and I got him to repair my boots, which he did. They were to last me all the way to America.

Tikal was magnificent—five great temples rising up through the jungle. Most of it was not cleared like it is now. If you want to see how it was when I was there, look at the *Star Wars* movie beginning, before the Stormtroopers attack the rebel army. The forest planet in that scene looks like, and is, Tikal. You can see the temples thrusting up through the jungle. We camped inside the ruins, which were free to enter, and other travelers who came through the day joined us. There was a small lake nearby, and I used it to bathe, wash my hair, and clean all of my clothes. I couldn't believe how soft my hair felt after the wash. That night, we all got stoned and slept under the stars. One guy had a guitar and could play really well. He played the Stones' song *Wild Horses*, and I can still vividly recall it to this day. It was all mind-blowing as we bedded down underneath one of the great temples.

The most amazing thing about the history of Tikal was that once the Mayans had built it, they all disappeared. No one could tell me where, but I suspect it was north into Mexico and the Yucatán Peninsula, where we were heading.

The next day, two New Yorkers, Sol and Carol, turned up in their camper van and befriended us. They were traveling around. Sol left me his New York telephone number and said to call when I reached town, which I did—but that was nearly six months later when I was on my way back to the UK. After a good night's sleep, we explored the ruins, and Sol and I climbed to the top of a temple, blew a joint, and couldn't get down again. We were up there nearly four hours, then tentatively eased down, and with some relief, collapsed when we got to the bottom. Never again. We had seen enough, and after one more night, we set our sights on Belize on the Caribbean coast.

Belize was once called British Honduras, and there was a distinct British manner about customs and immigration. Being on a British passport, I had no problems. We traveled by bus to the new capital city of Belize, Belmopan, but it was mainly a collection of new buildings with no significant atmosphere or people, for that matter. When I was in Houston, I went to the British Council to see if I could see a doctor for a gut complaint I had picked up in Mexico, and they asked me what Belmopan was like. They were a little aggrieved at my description. We left immediately for Belize City on the coast, and this was more like it. A collection of wooden buildings with the odd modern edifice, and for me, a British Council where I could read British newspapers and catch up with football scores.

The most startling thing was that there were a lot of Black African people walking the street, and I thought, probably because of past slavery history. The British had used slaves on their plantations, and of course, they had remained and were now a large part of the population. Hispanics and Brits were also evident, English was spoken in the street, and there was an English newspaper. Belize was famous mainly for the second-largest coral reef in the world, and most tourists came to see that. That didn't interest us, so we rested up and kept moving.

We hitched out to go north to Orange Walk and the Mexican border. A most astonishing thing happened. I was about 100 meters in front of Marcel, and as I approached customs, a woman came running out, threw her arms around me as though I was a long-lost lover. She then whispered to me that I should say I was her boyfriend, so I did. When we got through, she joined me and Marcel, and we walked away together. She then explained that the border officers were hassling her and wouldn't let her through. She said she was waiting for her boyfriend, and lo and behold, I was Johnny on the spot. Nothing came of the incident, but it emphasized the macho nature of Mexican men. I never saw her again. I thought she could have bought me a drink.

My aim at first was to hitch up the Yucatan coast to Isla Mujeres and Cancun, but after a day waiting and with no plans, we had to change our course. There was just no traffic on that road, so we went the other way and turned right on our way to the Mayan ruins at Chichen Itza and the city of Merida. Our first lift was astonishing, as it was a police car, and we accepted. The copper was going to Merida, and he was very friendly and hospitable. He asked questions about where we were going and where we had been. We mentioned New Zealand and

South America and that we were on our way to America, and he was quite taken with us. He lived in Merida, went to his home first, then took us back to Chichen Itza. We were relieved to get out of the car as he had brought up the subject of drugs, and of course, we said we had no part in it, as we were committed travelers. However, with me having shoulder-length hair, I think he was suspicious.

Chichen Itza was brilliant and, amazingly, like Tikal, it was free to get into. These days, I believe one pays $54US to get in. Like Tikal, it was only partly cleared, although there were more temples, dwellings, and a pelota court. Pelota was a basketball-like game, but legend had it that two brothers, who were gods, played it, and the loser had his head cut off; they then played with the head as a ball. There was a lot about sacrifice in Mayan culture, and one temple there was called the Temple of Skulls. There were skulls carved into the rock and stones from which it was made. There was also a cenote there—a deep sinkhole in the limestone rock that the Mayans used as a water supply. Needless to say, we stayed straight and went into Merida and found a pension for the night.

The next day was to be a long one, as we went to the other major Mayan ruin at Palenque and then hitched north towards Mexico City, aiming for the first Aztec stronghold at Tepoztlan. Palenque was well cleared, with a pelota court and a temple that had a big cellar in which was a black sculpture of a leopard with bright eyes. We had to pay to get into that, but paid nothing for the rest of the site. The pelota court was almost intact, but once again surrounded by stones with skulls carved into them. Much to think about, but now Aztec culture was our first priority, followed by Mexico City and the pyramids of the Sun and Moon at Teotihuacan, north of the city.

We hitched to Tepoztlan with a couple of American guys who were traveling around. They were in their 50s and, looking back, probably gay. But I was still naive about all that gay stuff, as it was rarely spoken about in those days. We arrived in Tepoztlan, an Aztec center and birthplace of the legendary feathered serpent, late in the evening. We had a bit of a worry when a group of Mexican lads invited us to stay at their place. We followed them for a while, and then they started up a hill. Marcel and I looked at each other. I asked if he was comfortable with this, and he said no. So we ran—with packs on our backs—to the bus station. The lads called after us but didn't give chase, though for a moment, we felt threatened.

Maybe we were wrong, but we didn't take risks. We changed our plans very quickly and took a night bus to Mexico City, staying in the bus depot until morning. Mexican buses were very modern and air-conditioned, unlike other buses we had been used to, and we vowed to use them until we got to America.

Mexico City was massive, but we made our way to Guerrero and found a pension that was majestic. It was built square, with three floors and a plaza with a garden in the middle. All the rooms looked out onto the plaza, and it was a shield from the mayhem in the streets of Mexico City. We shared the room with a very happy Japanese guy called Koji Okano. I read later that there was a Japanese film director of a similar name and wondered if he was the guy.

The important thing for me was that I had mail at the Poste Restante, which contained a bank statement saying money was available to me in Los Angeles, and this improved my morale like nothing else could at that moment in time. My parents were brilliant.

Teotihuacan was awe-inspiring. We walked down the Road of the Dead to the pyramids of the Sun and the Moon and stood atop both of them, breathing in the history that this place represented. It was at the heart of the Aztec civilization, but once again, the role of human sacrifice was evident. I wondered, why was this? The pyramids were unforgettable. With that in mind, it was back to Mexico City and a bus direct to the border town of Ciudad Juarez, across the Rio Grande from El Paso, which took a couple of days.

Ciudad Juarez was a wild town, and you had to watch everything, like it had been in Colombia. Lots of bars, girls hassling you for custom in the streets, pickpockets and thieves on every corner, and con men everywhere offering you paradise. "Hey, gringo" was a call I got sick of. I had to get out of here.

The next day, we crossed the Rio Grande to the border, and it was packed with vehicles going into the USA and people attempting entry, and that included us. The night before, we had cleaned up big time, including our backpacks, and wore our cleanest and best clothes. They separated us, and we were each interviewed by an immigration officer. The encounter I had with mine is one I will remember all my life.

I presented my passport, and in my best cockney, said that I wanted a transit visa to go to LA, then make my way to New York for a flight back to the UK. The immigration officer was a big, genial man with a Texas drawl, and he said a visa did not mean I had the right of entry. He asked me why I had gotten my visa in Bolivia. I said that I was traveling with an American at the time, and he told me that the Bolivian Embassy was quieter compared to the countries I was soon to travel in, and getting the visa there would improve my entry to other countries, knowing that I was going to America. He hummed and told me to empty my pockets and to drop my trousers. So I did. Mum had always said to wear a clean pair of underpants in case of events like this, and I had, and she was right. Nothing untoward. He told me to turn around, and then patted me down. He then asked why I had come through Mexico, and I told him I had started in South America, had a degree in history, and was interested in ancient civilizations like the Inca, Maya, and Aztecs. He seemed impressed and thawed a bit.

"What interests you in America?" he said. I muttered some codswallop about it being the leader of the free world and a must-see country. I particularly wanted to see the Grand Canyon. He said, "I will give you a 3-month transit visa," and stamped my passport. I smiled big time and thanked him very much. Marcel got something similar, but as it was late in the day, we decided to go back into Ciudad Juarez and cross the next day. That night was the best I had felt in a while, and the next day, we walked into El Paso.

First sight of South America. Tierra del Fuego 1972.

Plaza de Mayo Buenas Airies with Nico and Bekir.

89

Niteroi Beach Rio with Angelo, Juliane, Lydia and Roger 1972.

Indian women selling fish on shores of lake Titicaca Copacabana
Bolivia 1973.

Train from Cuzco to Machu Picchu 1973.

First view of Machu Picchu. I climbed the peak, it was easy. 1973.
The feeling up there is amazing.

Rescued by bulldozer after 4 hours near Puno Peru 1973. I have the knitted cap.

Boat down the Amazon. Slept on the deck. Others had hammocks.

Eating magic mushrooms San Augustine Colombia 1973 with Marcel on the left.

Sitting in both hemispheres Ecuador 1973.

Mayan Pelota court Copan Honduras 1973.

Trying to hitch a ride to Tikal Guatemala 1973 without success.

Temple 2 at Tikal. Camped just to the right. Very eerie. Climbed
another one stoned and couldn't getdown for sometime.

Mayan ruins at Palenque famous for an alleged 6ft 2inch astronaut
inside

Aztec Pyramid of the sun at Teotihuacan Mexico taken from atop
Pyramid of the Moon.

AMERICA

The Rio Grande River was not really a river. It was like a big drain, concreted over with a barbed wire fence on the American side. Texans called Mexicans "wetbacks" as they needed to swim the river to get into America, but we didn't need to swim. Customs was no problem, but thank heavens, there were no dogs, as the Colombian weed was still in the frame of my pack. As I walked into America, I sang Marty Robbins' song *"Out in the West Texas Town of El Paso..."* I was happy to be in America.

The first week in America—or should I say Texas? Because in Texas, it's Texas first, America second—was one of the most memorable of all my travel experiences. It started when we walked into El Paso, and because it was hot and sunny, and we were in cowboy country, I decided to buy a cowboy hat. Now, I don't wear a hat well, but I threw caution to the wind and bought a wide-brimmed hat. I immediately put it on my head and walked around like a gunslinger, then walked to the start of Route 40 to Las Cruces. While standing at the side of the road near a gas station, a man walked up to me and said that it was the Lord's day, and I should reconsider whether I wanted to hitchhike on his day. I didn't reply, although I was sorely tempted. The religious underbelly of America had made itself known very early in my stay.

It took a while to get a ride, but it took us to Las Cruces, which was a fair ride. Then we were immediately picked up by a woman in a Ute-like vehicle who asked us where we were going. I said, in my best Cockney, "The Grand Canyon," because that was a priority, and she said she was having a party that night and would we like to come? We did, so it was off to her place, where there were quite a few people already drinking and toking up, so we joined them. The woman had lived in London in the late 60s, was a fan of Led Zeppelin, and had visited the Marquee Club, and she just wanted to talk about it. So we did. We were popular guests, so we decided to stay the night and slept outside on the verandah.

The next morning, we were up early and on the road to Albuquerque. It was tough going, and we felt that motorists were deterred by the fact that there were two of us, so we decided to split up and meet at the Grand Canyon. I left Marcel where we were, and I walked a couple of hundred meters down the road. He got picked up soon after, and he waved as he went by, and that was the last I saw of him. I have tried to trace him since, without luck. I hope he was and is OK. I, on the other hand, had one of the scariest times of my life. I was picked up by a guy who turned out to be an ex-soldier who had served some time in Vietnam and had had some early training at Colchester, England, as a young soldier before being deployed in Berlin. I was chatting away like nobody's business when I looked down and saw he had a gun under his right leg. It worried me, and I said, "I notice you have a gun; you have nothing to be scared of with me."

He seemed OK, but I was on edge. Then he decided to stop at a layby off the highway for a rest. No sooner had he stopped than I opened the door and shot away quick, with my pack still in the back seat of his car. He got out, and I couldn't see the gun. He called out to me, "Five minutes." I said, "Fine," and had a leak. I sauntered wearily back, and he was OK. I said, "I think I'll get out here," but he insisted on taking me to the next town, which was Winslow, Arizona, and he let me off there. But I was shit scared and ultra-wary from then on.

I walked through Winslow, and it was full of Indians who were lying around. I found out from my next ride that it was treaty money day, and they had all come to town. My thoughts, as I write this piece, are with the Eagles song that goes, "I was standing on the corner in Winslow, Arizona, such a fine sight to see." I was shattered but got back on the road and had luck almost immediately from a young guy who was going back home to Los Angeles. He was, as they say, totally cool, and I relaxed. He told me Los Angeles could be pretty bad, and I would have to watch myself. After what had just happened, I was a bit apprehensive. He dropped me off at the turn-off to the Grand Canyon in the late afternoon, and the day got suddenly better.

I figured I would have to stay outdoors for the night, so I stashed my pack well off the road at a place I would recognize again, and walked down to a house a ways down the road and asked for some water. They were great and gave me a plastic bottle full, and I started back to my pack when a camper van stopped and asked me where I was going. I said the Grand Canyon, but my pack was down the road. The young lady who was driving said, "Go get it," and I did.

Her name was Susie, and she was from California. She was accompanied by her young cousin Johnny and his mate Mark. We chatted, and she told me she had lived in London, and said that she was going to Houston to see her older cousin, who was getting married, and hopefully to work. Food for thought, I was prepared to change direction after hearing about L.A.

The Grand Canyon was brilliant and not the over-controlled, consumer rat race that it is now. I know this because my family and I visited it again in 2017. I stayed the night, sleeping outside next to Susie's motorbike, and the next day explored the Canyon in all its magnificence. We all got on great, and they asked if I wanted to come with them to Houston. I thought about the money in the bank in L.A. and what the young guy had said about L.A., and said, "OK." It was one of the best decisions I ever made, and after the last couple of days, I started to feel safe and welcome.

Houston.

When we arrived in Houston, we went to stay with Susie's cousin Danny in an apartment complex in Long Point. Danny was about 2 meters tall and stayed with little Danny, with whom he had served in Vietnam. They were great guys, and big Danny was going to marry little Danny's sister Josie in San Antonio at the end of the week. I also met Big Danny's parents, Will, who was about 2 meters tall as well, and a lovely little lady, his wife Billie. I got on like a house on fire with Billie, and she mothered me. She got me to do jobs around her house, like the lawns and garden, and paid me for it.

I stayed a couple of days with Will and Billie, and we went up to their holiday home in Centreville before heading on to see the prison Rodeo at Huntsville prison. Male and female prisoners roped calves, rode bulls and bucking broncos, and did all the rodeo things within the prison grounds. Unique. Will was an immigration officer and offered to help me out if I wanted to stay. I considered it, but no. I needed to get money fast, so I walked around Long Point and saw a sign outside a car wash: *Help Wanted.* I went in, got the job, and the next day started washing cars one after the other, all day long. The pay was poor, but my employer asked me for my Social Security number, which I didn't have, of course. So, I applied to Maryland where all that was handled, and within a fortnight, I had a Social Security card and number. I could work legally.

After a couple of weeks, I was in a position to make decisions about what I was going to do. Big Danny's wedding took Susie away, and Johnny and Mark were sent back to L.A. on the bus. I looked after their flat while they were all gone and got on very well with the tenants in the other apartments. They invited me out to a party and a nightclub, but I had no clothes to wear, so they clubbed together and gave me a very 70's outfit to wear – platform shoes, bell-bottomed pants that were tight, and a floral shirt. I looked like a fruitcake but had a fun time. When Susie came back, she acted unsettled, and I thought I had overstayed my welcome, so I decided to hit the road again. I was wrong, and she asked me to stay.

The next day, we went on a road trip back the way we had come, with me on the back of Susie's bike. We went through all those places, like the Painted Desert, that Peter Fonda and Dennis Hopper crossed in

Easy Rider, with Jack Nicholson on the back. The mission was to see a property that her father had bought as an investment. It was just a piece of land with nothing around it, but clearly, future plans would take place. A couple of photographs, then back to Houston.

Susie got a job at Texas Instruments, a technology company, and met a girl called Belinda who had an apartment and needed a flatmate. She asked me to come, so I quit the car wash and moved into a Beechnut flat on the other side of Houston. I got a job as a short-order cook at Long John Silver's Fish and Chips, and we settled into domestic bliss. Belinda had a little boy, about 15 months old and walking around. He took a shine to me and followed me everywhere—so did Belinda, but I kept her at bay. Susie wanted us to go through the dating thing, and this meant going to places and dinners, etc. So, I went along with it, and we did some amazing things.

We saw a concert by Tom Jones, at which women threw their knickers up on stage. Tom would wipe his brow and throw them back, resulting in a great scramble in the crowd. He also explained the word *indubitably*, which in Texan meant *No Shit*—a phrase Texans use all the time. The best concert was by Liza Minnelli, who performed songs from *Cabaret* with two male dancers and a chair. It was wonderful, and it evoked memories of the film I saw in Peru. Then there was the Charlie Rich, Mack Davis, ZZ Top concert before the beards, which was emotive. Texans sang their hearts out to *Behind Closed Doors* by Charlie Rich and laughed at Mack Davis's *Lord, It's Hard to Be Humble*. Unforgettable.

I also went to a baseball game with the Atlanta Braves playing the Houston Astros at the Astrodome, featuring Hank Aaron, the man who was to beat Babe Ruth's home run record. I saw the Houston Oilers play the New York Jets in American football, featuring the all-American hero Joe Namath as quarterback. I was living the American dream. Then came the most famous event of all, also at the

Astrodome: the Battle of the Sexes tennis match between Bobby Riggs and Billie Jean King, in which Billie Jean thrashed Riggs, who was little more than a braggart. But the good times were coming to an end.

I was restless. I had enjoyed making fish and chips and had built up a clientele of people who came to eat my fish and chips. It was amazing; I even got tips. I also got on very well with the boss, who loved fast cars and once drove me at over 100 mph on the motorway and had me over to dinner with his family. Unfortunately, I blew that when his mother asked me if I would come to church with them, and I said I wasn't a believer. That religious underbelly again. I decided I was going. I had overstayed my 3-month transit visa and didn't fancy being caught out and confined in America. I told Susie I was going to New York, and she convinced me not to hitchhike but to take the plane, which I did. I landed at JFK Airport, New York City, and telephoned Sol and Carol, who I had met at Tikal in Guatemala. Sol was a taxi driver, and he picked me up and took me to their controlled-rent apartment on 33rd Street, Manhattan, and a new adventure started.

I stayed a week in New York and did all the tourist things—Empire State Building, Statue of Liberty, Central Park, Greenwich Village, et al. At night, I took Sol and Carol's dog for a walk in Central Manhattan, and it was a sight to see. Not always safe, but having the dog gave me confidence. I wish I had gone up the Twin Towers, but there was a queue. Too late now. I did like New York and returned in 2016 with my wife and granddaughters, enjoying it all over again.

I saw an advertisement in the Village Voice for a cheap flight to London via Iceland and Glasgow with Icelandic Airlines. I bought a ticket and left. I wondered what immigration would say about overstaying, but they were good about it. I said I loved being here and was sorry to go. So, back to London to save for an African journey.

Grand Canyon. One of the most impressive natural wonders I ever saw.

Madison Avenue New York from inside Sol's taxi cab on the way to Central park.

LONDON (1973-74)

The good thing about being back in London was that I didn't have to be a cockney anymore. Not that I didn't like Cockneys, it's just that I am a kiwi guy and I preferred that. Ironically, though, the first thing I did off the plane at Heathrow was to go out to Upton Park to watch West Ham play. I was in heaven, but I had an alternative reason, as I had to pick up a bag I had left with a mate, Alan, before I left to go overland to New Zealand three years previously.

Alan lived in one of those blocks of flats that overlooks Upton Park. He had wanted to come with me when I left in 1971 but had developed epilepsy and couldn't travel. He was pleased to see me and dragged my bag from a back cupboard, and I was off to Kingston Upon Thames where my old mucker and fellow traveller, Harry, lived.

I stayed at his place for the night and, the next day, found a bedsit in Minerva Road near the Fairfield Recreation Ground. I was to be happy living there, and thanks to Harry, I got a job at Vine Products Winery just down the road, where the office accounts clerk was also a West Ham fan. His name was Morris, and he was the worst darts player I had ever met in my life. I called him "Keep it Friendly Morris" because he lost us so many matches, but he was great company at the West Ham games.

We did have one eventful trip by train to Leicester with the West Ham fans, but a few of them smashed up their carriage—fortunately, not the one we were in. At Leicester, they stopped the train before the station, ordered everybody out, and we faced a line of police on horseback all the way to the ground. We vowed, "Never again!" and didn't catch the train back, preferring to wait for a later train, which got us back to London about midnight. We managed to get the last Tube train to Richmond and walked the rest of the way to Kingston

Upon Thames. We had Richmond Park on our left, and deer came out to play. It was wonderful; I will never forget.

I worked at Vine Products filtering wine and was able to work six days a week and have a social life as well as save a bit aside for an African adventure. Then I made a decision I regretted. A girl named Kris, who I had been friendly with before I left for South America, decided she wanted to come to London and asked if she could stay with me. I said yes because I had stayed with plenty of folk during my travels. It wasn't that she was a bad chick; it was just that travelling like I did required a bit of verve, and she didn't have it. She was a farmer's daughter and had a bit of brass, so there were compensations.

She settled in, and I told her about my planned African journey and suggested she and another New Zealand girl go on a European trip to test themselves and see great things. She agreed and went, but she would be back.

In the meantime, I had a ball. Bowie was big in London, and everything was androgynous, and my favourite album was *Astral Weeks* by Van Morrison. The thing about London, and Britain as a whole, is that everybody knows their music. The pubs are full of it, and wherever you go, the music was incredible. Not far from Kingston, going towards Richmond, there was a pub called the Greyhound that had a jazz night on Sundays. I saw some fabulous people play there, none of them household names, but the music was superb.

Kris returned. I had met someone else, but she discussed Africa, and I knew she had money, so the new girl was gone, and we planned for Africa. On the eve of our departure, I received a telegram from home saying my father was seriously ill in hospital, was expected to die, and that I shouldn't come home because of it. I was saddened and sent a return telegram saying I was hoping for the best.

On 13th July 1974, we took a train to Southampton and a boat to Cherbourg in France, and the African trip was underway.

AFRICA (July 1974 - January 1975)

It didn't take long for the difference between Kris and me to show itself, and it was perfectly understandable. I wasn't adept enough at caring for a woman; I was used to it being only me. I was a hardened traveller; I could sleep anywhere and live off the smell of an oily rag. She, on the other hand, needed all the easy things in life: a bed, a shower, a good meal, and comfort. I couldn't afford these on the road, and knowing the distance we had to go, I was frugal at best. It was the beginning of an explosive relationship, but it wasn't all bad—we had some brilliant times, as you will read about.

First day hitchhiking off the Cherbourg ferry was grim. We got to Caen and bedded down outside behind a hedge. The next day was better but not great. We got to Chateau de Loire and camped outside for a second night. There was a lake, and I swam and cleaned up; Kris didn't. It was starting to get testy.

The next day was brilliant. We were picked up by an Aussie called Peter who was driving a truck to Morocco, and we hoped he would take us all the way—and he nearly did. We crossed into Spain, found a pension for the night, had a hot shower and a meal, and things were hunky-dory.

The next day, we drove all the way to Algeciras, which overlooked Gibraltar across the bay. Brilliant view, so we got a hotel which was too dear, stayed the night, and prepared for a ferry to Tangier in Morocco. Customs and immigration on leaving Spain were a hassle, and I was glad to leave, but boarding the ferry became a huge argument. Our Aussie driver had come down with a stomach complaint and couldn't drive the truck onto the ferry. Although I had driven a bus in Afghanistan, I couldn't handle a truck, so I looked to Kris to drive. I knew she was a good driver, and under the circumstances, she could have stepped up—but she refused. The

Aussie ordered us off the truck, and that was the end of a good ride into Morocco.

We arrived in Tangier at night and walked through a deserted town looking for a place to stay. Kris was nervous, so we took the first hotel we found. was too dear but what the fuck. I enjoyed walking around Tangier—the Berber and Arabic culture and economy were interesting. Women were almost invisible, as they had been in Afghanistan, and this increased the pressure on Kris, who walked around in tight jeans and loose tops. I would have too.. But the men couldn't handle that, and she was continually banged into and touched as we walked around. This occurred all the way across North Africa and, understandably, did not make Kris happy. We couldn't walk side by side, so I got her to walk in front while I kept vigil from behind.

Our first port of call was Asilah, an alleged surfing and hippy spot on the Atlantic coast with a lovely beach—but it turned out not to be that at all. We saw few foreigners but managed to spend a couple of days on the beach away from the fishing boats that beached at night. Sleeping outside was not an option, so we got a cheap hotel, which wasn't cheap by Asian and South American standards. I realised this was going to be a more expensive trip than the others I had been on.

Back to Tangier and a train to Casablanca, which was memorable because we got hit by a dust storm coming in from the desert. The train was engulfed in sand and dust, and we had to cover our mouths and noses to stop inhaling the cursed stuff. This was to happen to us again on a train trip in the Sudan, and it is not pleasant. We always carried water bottles and used chlorine tablets in case of disease, but we rapidly went through water as it was very hot. Our hair and clothes got covered, and it was a rather bedraggled pair that got off the train in Casablanca and went straight to a hotel at any cost.

Something happened during our stay in Casablanca that I wasn't attuned to at the time, but on looking back and reading my diary, it seems obvious to me—and had a dramatic effect on Kris. The pension where we stayed was run by two young men who were ultra-friendly from the start. Normally I am suspicious of this but somehow dropped my guard. After wandering around Casablanca all day looking for Rick's Bar without success, we retired to our room, only to get a knock on the door asking if I wanted to have a drink of whisky. As a Scot, I naturally said yes, but they didn't want Kris involved. I should have clicked but didn't. I got shitfaced, and when I returned to our room, Kris was testy and upset. I thought it was me and forgot about it. Kris never talked about it, but she was out of sorts and sick for much of our journey across North Africa.

We rose early, skipped paying the bill, and buggered off to the railway station, catching the train to Marrakesh. "Do you know we're riding on the Marrakesh Express, they're taking me to Marrakesh. All aboard that train." It was a lovely train journey, and Kris seemed OK.

Marrakesh was brilliant. We got a cheap hotel in Fa'anna Square called the Hillal at 10 dirham a night. It was a bargain. We washed all our clothes and spent three days relaxing here. I scored some good weed, and tensions eased markedly, so I thought things were alright. But looking back, I may have been wrong, and perhaps Kris had been sexually assaulted. I will never know because I cannot trace her anywhere. We did meet after I arrived back in New Zealand, but no meaningful conversation took place, as I was facing a drugs charge in which she was implicated—but that is another story.

After a day trip to the desert kasbah of Quarzazate, we took a succession of buses north to Meknes, Fez, and east to Oujda and the Algerian border. The Algerian customs and immigration took us apart, but I never carried contraband these days, so we started hitching and got picked up by two Japanese guys who were driving to Algiers. We spent a happy time singing and laughing our way to the Algerian capital. It was obvious that Algeria was better off than

Morocco—and more expensive too—but Algiers was a modern French city and good to walk around. However, Kris was still hassled in the streets.

We decided to move quickly to Tunisia, catching a bus through the Atlas Mountains to Constantine and thence to the Tunisian border, where we got stuck along with several other western travellers. But it was great to share experiences and enjoy the company. After a couple of days, the banks opened, we could change money, and we took a bus straight to Tunis city and the ruins of Carthage, which I was looking forward to seeing.

Tunis city was very relaxing and interesting—and, more importantly, cheap. We had a good room in our hotel with a double bed and a hot shower. It was great to be clean again, and the food was also a cut above what we had gotten in Morocco and Algeria. The ruins at Carthage, where Dido and Hannibal had frequented, were not as impressive as others I had seen—but just being there was moving. The thing that impressed me about Tunisians was their open friendliness; there wasn't the hassle for Kris that there had been in Morocco and Algeria. It was here that we found out Nixon had resigned as president after the Watergate scandal, and all that day, people would come up to us and tell us. I was delighted, of course— it was good news in a troubled world.

We had business to do here as we had decided to go across Libya to Egypt and we needed to get our passports translated into Arabic for Libya, and Kris needed a visa for Egypt as she was on a New Zealand passport. This was all acquired, and we went south to El Djem, where there was an almost complete colosseum similar to the one in Rome. Although it was smaller, we were allowed to walk through it. We could also stay in the waiting room at the lovely railway station, which was free, and await the bus for the Libyan border. There were other travellers there doing what we wanted to do, and we moved as a group to Libya. No problems getting to the border, but then it was a long, hot, dusty bus journey to Tripoli and Gaddafi's Libya.

On arrival at the bus station, we looked around, and all the signage on the streets was in Arabic—there was no English translation anywhere. We were a group of about ten people but all very "hippyfied," and we soon attracted unwanted attention. We were befriended by a couple of Palestinian guys who spoke good English, and they took us to a place to stay but warned us not to venture out at night or alone. Discussion at night was alarmist, and I didn't fancy travelling in Libya after these initial happenings. So we took a bus straight out to the airport, which was quite modern. Libya obviously was a richer country than the ones we had just left, but westerners were not popular. We bought tickets to Cairo for about $140 US each, which was $40 more expensive than for a Libyan national. We were glad to go—Egypt and the pyramids awaited.

Egypt was an emotional time for me. After we had found a cheap hotel in Tahrir Square, I went to poste restante for my mail and found two letters from home: one from my brother Drew and one from my sister-in-law Lynne, to tell me my father had died. I expected it and had prepared myself for it, but when it actually hits you, it is a blow. I didn't always get on with my father, but he was my dad, and I respected what he had done in his life.

It was also emotional in that the hotel we found was full of travellers like myself, and the old camaraderie that I had found in my travels to Asia and South America was back. We were on the second floor, and it overlooked Tahrir Square—a massive place with overhead walkways for pedestrians and hectic traffic on the roads underneath. We could see the Hilton Hotel by a bridge over the Nile, and to our right was the road to the fabulous Egyptian Museum. In spite of my grief, I was also happier than at any time on the road so far. And the best thing was it was dirt cheap to stay there—about $1 US a day. As we walked around Cairo, many Egyptians would come up to us and say thank you for coming to see their country. I put this down to the fact that troubles in the region had deterred tourists and travellers, as this same friendliness was not there when I came back to Cairo in 2007 with my wife Celia. We couldn't find the hotel I stayed in during 1974, and all the overhead walkways had gone. Tahrir Square was a free-for-all for Egyptian drivers, and the Hilton was called something else.

The bus to Giza and the pyramids left from Tahrir Square, and we got there early in the morning when hardly anyone was around. I climbed the Cheops, something you cannot do now, and walked right around the Sphinx, which you cannot do now either. It was quite a hard climb, as the stones were very big, and much of the time I was on my hands and knees. People bellowed at me to stop, but I persisted, and the view from the top was superb. I thought I would cop it when I came down, but nothing happened, so I went about my business like nothing was wrong.

The thing about Egypt that makes it a must-visit is that all the ruins and monuments you see deliver, and the next place we were to go, Luxor, proves this point overwhelmingly. It was awe-inspiring, but getting there was a big hassle, especially the 16-hour train journey to Luxor. Getting tickets for the train was just as bad as in India. Then we had to run across the tracks to ensure we got a seat in the third-class section. We didn't, but a very kind guard came over to us, shook his head, and then led us into the second-class section, and that is where we stayed for the whole dusty journey.

In Luxor, we stayed at the Station Hotel, which was cheap, but the streets were crammed with people who were skilled at dealing with tourists. We visited Karnak, walked between the tall columns, swam in the Nile, ate in the market, bought a delicious melon, then went back to the hotel. It was very hot. We were appalled at the treatment donkeys got from their owners. They were loaded up with commodities and whipped if they stopped, but you daren't say anything.

The next day we were off on another train journey to Aswan and checked in at the youth hostel. The train journey took five hours, and it was something else. The Nile river was beautiful—picture-postcard stuff—and arrival at Aswan came quickly. Everywhere there were signs telling us "no photographs" because of the dam, which couldn't be seen from the station or the town. We caught a felucca to Elephantine Island, which has a memorial to Agha Khan, who was well known in racing circles and upper-class social circles in the UK. We signed the visitors' book, smoked a joint, and then made our way back. It was a great night, as there were many travellers waiting to take the boat down Lake Nasser to Wadi Halfa. We loaded up with supplies for the boat trip, which was to take two days and nights and pass the great temple of Abu Simbel in the middle of the first night.

To get on the boat, we had to go through immigration for the Sudan, with our vaccination certificates closely scrutinised for yellow fever and cholera. That took time, but we managed, along with other travellers, to get a good space on the top deck where we gazed at the desert all day under a marijuana cloud. Nobody bothered us, which was surprising. We passed Abu Simbel at about 3 o'clock in the morning, but it was worth the wait. The giant statues of Rameses II stood out, and it was a shame we could not stop.

Wadi Halfa wasn't the metropolis we expected, and we had to walk 2–3 kilometres through the desert to get to the train station, but the train to Khartoum was waiting, and the journey was one to remember. It was a steam train and needed to stop to take on water from time to time, with black smoke pouring out of the engine into the wide, expansive rocky desert that surrounded us. All the foreigners got up on the roof and had a ball until we saw a familiar dust cloud rapidly coming our way. We scrambled inside as the dust storm engulfed the whole train, getting into everything. You couldn't see the end of the carriage—the dust was so thick. It was most uncomfortable, but we knew from our Moroccan experience how to cope.

As the dust cloud passed, we saw smaller villages with black people, many with scarred faces that indicated the tribe they belonged to. Until now, it had been all Arabic, but now we knew we were in black Africa, although Arabic faces still dominated. We arrived at Abu Hamed, a small town, and black people sold us mangoes and figs and tea, of all things, which was delicious. The train hit the Nile shortly after, and at a place called Atbara, we changed from our steam train to a diesel train, and the carriages got more crowded.

At Khartoum, the dirtiest pack of travellers I have ever seen in my life got off the train and made their way to the youth hostel, only to encounter a very officious young man who would only allow those with the green International Youth Hostel card to stay at the hostel. We got together and said, "OK, none of us will stay here," and he backed down and was quite helpful after that. The power of the group was inspirational, and I doubt that many could say they ever experienced that reaction. "Power to the People," as John Lennon once sang.

Khartoum was a disappointment. Dusty, dirty, and lacking in character, it was difficult to see why the British had fought major battles over this place. We had business to do here, however, as we needed a visa to Zaire and a permit to travel further south to Malakal and Juba because there were rebel armies in the region. The war to separate from Sudan had begun this far back. We also needed to negotiate a student discount for the train and boat journey along the Nile, which was to take 13 days and finish in Juba. We had three days to wait in Khartoum and decided to cross the river to Omdurman, quietly known as the biggest camel market in the world—and it was. Then it was back to the youth hostel to lie down and read. I was reading *Mill on the Floss* by George Eliot and thoroughly enjoyed it. The company we kept was mainly English guys, and we had fun and smoked a lot of gockle.

The train journey came, and the impact was amazing. We now knew we were really in black Africa, as everybody except us travellers was black, and it was crowded. It was hot and sticky in the carriage, so the roof was the most appealing place to be—so up we went. There was something quite exhilarating about being on the roof of a train, and I thought of one of my favourite songs: "When the sun beats down and melts the tar up on the roof." It was wide enough and safe enough to sleep up there, so we did, and when we woke, it was to lush greenery with small villages splattered along the way. This was the Africa I had dreamed of.

We arrived at Kosti on the White Nile, and the rush was incredible. Everybody ran like the wolf was after them to get on the boat. Pushing and shoving, we embarked and claimed our territory on the deck because we were going to live here for the next 13 days. Having established our demesne, we went ashore for supplies and water because the boat did not supply these cheaply, although it did have tea and meals in the first-class section of the boat—but these were far too expensive for my budget. The Africans were very good and invited us to share their meals, mainly composed of dried meat and a sago-type mush, much like porridge. It was good, and we gave them money, which they didn't ask for but were grateful to receive.

We were travelling upriver, so progress was slow and got even slower as we ran into weed-like water lilies that went from bank to bank and piled up in the bow of the boat. The toilets became clogged with shit, attracting flies, and the smell was horrible. They were cleaned at night and then filled up again. At night, the mosquitoes were in their element, and I realised that I would need to buy a mosquito net before travelling further into Africa.

We decided to eat first class so we could use their toilet. This was expensive, but our health was at stake, so what the hell. A tropical storm hit one night, so we had to get up, pack our things, and stand under the canvas shelter. Many got waterlogged, but it did wash the decking down, and that had to be a good thing. This was tough travelling, but the travellers on board stayed cool.

We stopped at Malakal, which was a collection of shacks, and many passengers got off the boat, enabling us travellers to swap sides of the boat. The river narrowed after this, and we saw more life on the banks—primitive at that. We saw kids naked and covered in ashes but wondered where all the crocodiles were, as they were famous on this river. Friday the 13th of September came, and, as befitted this day, the boat hit a sandbank and got stuck. At night, the mosquitoes were thicker than a London fog, so we covered all parts of our bodies and hoped for the best.

Three days later, we got to Juba in the dark, tried to find a hotel, but they were all booked, so we had to camp at the police station. One of our number was very sick with malaria and was hospitalised. I was feeling like shit and very loose in the bowels, but we needed to register, get a Zaire visa, and get permission to travel south to the Zaire border. We heard about a mission a few kilometres out of town, so we walked there, and after telling a tall story in my schoolboy French, they let us stay. The room was clean, had mosquito screens, and a clean toilet. It was heaven, but I was on the loo all night and could "shit through a needle" at will.

The next three weeks or so were the hardest travelling that I had ever done. Kris and I were very sick and, strangely, very cold, but we had to go on—and we did. It was a remarkable effort. We got an express bus to Yei along a dirt road, passed customs and police checks, then caught a truck across into Zaire to a place called Aba, where we camped down in a deserted building with a veranda and a water tank. Nobody said anything, so we stayed the night. I was feverish and still had the shits, and Kris was not well either. I feared having amoebic dysentery, so I went to a doctor in a health centre and used my schoolboy French to outline the problem. The doctor was Belgian-trained and sorted me out with some pills to stop the perpetual bowel movements, and it cost me about $5 US. On returning to our accommodation, a bugle sounded, and they started to play the national anthem. Police and soldiers were around, so we stood respectfully and watched as a poor man on a bicycle, who didn't stop, was dragged from his bike and beaten mercilessly by the soldiers. This was Mobutu's Zaire, and he was a noted tyrant. He added the words "Sese Seko" to his name, which meant "Mobutu forever and ever," and you crossed him at your peril.

After seeing this, we discussed whether it was worth travelling in Zaire at all, but the alternative was crossing into Uganda, which was ruled by a worse tyrant, Idi Amin. So we decided to continue south to Bunia near the Rwanda border, then onto Goma with a chance to see the gorillas. The road to Bunia was horrendous, and the bus was carrying dried fish bales, which we had to sit on. At times, we had to get out of the bus—or "fulla fulla," as they called it—so that we could pass other buses on a road that was narrow and muddy, and the fulla fulla slid from side to side in the squelching mud. We got two punctures, and the tyres had to be changed; meanwhile, we stood outside in the pouring rain, hungry, tired, cold, and shitting through the eye of a needle. The Africans were good-humoured about it all.

They were small people compared to us, with broad smiles that brightened up our misery. We got to Bunia only to be told that the road to Goma was closed for at least 18 days, so it was either go back the way we came or go inland to Kisangani, take a train to Ubanda, a boat trip down the Congo to Kindu, and a train trip to Kalemie on Lake Victoria for a ship ride to Tanzania. How many people today could—or would—put up with that? Us boomers were lucky bastards, alright, and it was to get worse.

The road from Bunia to Kisangani was little more than a red dirt gash through the jungle with no sealing. It got really squelchy after rain and was barely wide enough for two trucks to get past each other when travelling in opposite directions. I learned two things about Zaire on this trip.

Firstly, that the truck driver is king. He does what he likes and sets the price of the fare, and in this instance, it was an expensive 10 Zaire each. Secondly, nothing moves unless it is carrying beer. Beer is the other king, and the truck we were on was loaded with it, and sitting on top of crates was sore-bum material, big time.

We made good time at first and got to a place called Mambasa where the driver decided to have a drink, so we did too. The trip had been interesting as we saw Pygmies, and I bought a Coca-Cola off one at an exorbitant 20 Zaire because my guts were not good, and experience told me coke would fix it, and it did. Then it started to rain, and it pissed down. We got back on the truck and covered ourselves with a ground sheet. The blacks on the truck got drenched but didn't bat an eyelid—this was everyday stuff to them. Then we met a truck that was sideways across the road, so no-one could pass, and it was stuck in the mud. Everybody off the truck while the men dug the stuck truck out and got it to move. Our truck followed slowly for about 200 meters; then we got back on and made our way to Bafwasende where I bought a nice-smelling meal wrapped in broad leaves with lots of juice in it. It tasted good with the manioc, but I later found out that it was monkey. Not to worry—ebola had not been discovered then.

We slept on top of the truck with everybody, fitfully at best, but it was an early morning start, and we arrived at Kisangani in the late afternoon. There, we met two American guys who were going our way and had got permission to stay in the local Mission School gymnasium and invited us along. It was bliss. We had a cold shower, cleaned up, and went walkies after locking our gear away in a closet. We went looking to change money as there was a thriving black market in Zaire and found an Italian Chemist who gave us favourable rates. It was quite a relief as we were broke. We met quite a few travellers, and by night-time, there were about ten of us in the gym, and we had quite a session. It was the best I had felt in a while, and Kris was well too.

Next day we walked around Kisangani and saw a white Mongol African, which was quite a rarity because part of the mumbo jumbo that permeates this place believes that eating Mongol bones is a powerful healer, and many are killed because of it. The houses and shops were little more than shacks, although there were some impressive homes. Mobutu propaganda was everywhere. One more night in the gym, then across the river to catch a very slow train to Poitierville or Ubundu as it is known now, which took nine hours, with the jungle at places growing right across the track. We found a mission, and it had a beautiful room with a cold outside shower, but the weather was warm, and we used the time well to wash all our clothes and rest. The Monsignor invited us to dinner, and it was a luxuriant spread that gladdened our hearts after all we had been through.

A very sobering experience happened to me as I was bringing in the washing, which I had hung on a line from a wardrobe to an outside post. As I reached to take my jeans down, I found myself looking into the eyes of a green mamba snake, its eyes boring into me, its tongue flicking in and out. Then he suddenly slithered down the back of the wardrobe, and I ran for it, but he shot into the long grass and was off. I called out "snake!" and a black African woman went for it with a panga or large knife, and I sat down and thanked my lucky stars as they are poisonous.

The next morning we boarded the boat that was to take us to Kindu along the Congo River, and naturally, it was carrying beer as a cargo. It was little more than a barge with two motorboats, one on each side, and progress upstream was slow. Photography was strictly forbidden, even though for much of the journey, we hogged one side or the other. Zaire is a very paranoid country with the power of Mobutu obvious everywhere in an oversensitive way. The first day was quite relaxed as the travellers claimed their space on the deck, and at night we could buy a beer, smoke a bit of bhang, and watch the sun go down very quickly. The people were not friendly at all, especially the women, and the hygiene on the boat was no better than elsewhere, with the toilet full of shit after about half a day. We did see lots of hippos in the river but no crocodiles. There was plenty of birdlife.

We arrived at Kindu just after 1.00 pm and were the first off the truck and started walking into the town to find a hotel, but they were all full. We stopped at the market to buy some fruit and whatever else we could eat, and things went pear-shaped very quickly. The cost of things was nearly double what it was in Kisangani, and we haggled, which the people didn't like. Kids started throwing things at us, so we raced towards the mission house. The local crowd, sensing blood, joined in, and we were lucky to get through the front doors into the mission. When the crowd pushed that down, we got through the next doors into the heart of the mission. Staff from the mission came out to cool the crowd down and disperse them, and I have to admit I was shit-scared. The mission didn't want us there, but we had a French couple with us, and they argued our case with the Monsignor, and he allowed us to stay. As the night went on, we discovered that this area had been subject to European mercenaries during the civil war in Katanga and Zaire, and many untoward things had been done by them. Europeans were not popular, and we suffered the consequences.

The next morning we were up early and down to the station to catch the train to Kalemie on Lake Tanganyika for a crossing to Tanzania and out of this godforsaken country.

Unfortunately, it wasn't over yet, and the train only took us to Kongolo, where we luckily caught another train immediately to Kalemie. We didn't know this when we bought the tickets, but that is Africa, and the train to Kalemie was a breeze compared to other travel in Zaire. We bought cooked fish in broad green leaves, manioc, and fruit along the way, and at a station called Kabalo, the excellent cafeteria served tea and bread, and we were in heaven. I felt the sickness start to leave me and looked forward to crossing Lake Tanganyika to Kigoma, but it still wasn't over, and there was to be drama in which a border guard held a gun to my head.

We hadn't realised that our Zaire visas had expired by one day. Most of that delay was due to the erratic travel services within this country, so we had some explaining to do. We knew that our finances would be scrutinised because we had to fill a form in when we entered the country and show currency exchanges when we left. We had only used a bank once in Zaire, and that dealing was stamped in my passport — fortunately, because our financial papers had been lost.

Once in Kalemie, we bought tickets for the lake crossing and paid by travellers' cheque. All the cash we had was rolled up in the sleeves of the shirt that I used to cross borders in. On boarding the boat, we went through a very aggressive customs and immigration process, who accused us of everything. I denied it vehemently, and it was then that a gun was held to my head. It was frightening because life was very cheap in this part of the world, and I am not a brave man at the best of times. We explained that we had lived cheaply and had stayed at missions for free. We had no intention of ripping the Zaire Republic and its people off. We showed the travellers' cheque receipts for the boat tickets and explained that travellers' cheques were the only money we had. They left us alone for a while, then came back to tell us we could board the ship. The relief was immense, and later that day we left for Kigoma.

The overnight boat ride was pleasant, and we landed in Kigoma with the plan of crossing the Serengeti but found we had to go to Musoma through another port town, Mwanza, to do this. Kigoma was a miserable place, but there were a lot of Asian traders, and we changed money at an advantageous rate so that our life in Julius Nyerere's African Socialist state was easier. But it wasn't.

On the train, Kris had her watch ripped off her arm, and we decided then that 3rd class train travel was no longer an option and upped it to 2nd class, where we could sleep in safety. Mwanza was on Lake Victoria, and a massive lake it was, like a sea rather than a lake, as was Lake Tanganyika. We then moved on to Musoma by train, and it was a delightful place on Lake Victoria, where we paid for a bus to cross the Serengeti. We also paid 23 shillings each for a guided trip down the Ngorongoro Crater, cleaned up at a very good boarding house, and had a good meal. After Zaire, this was paradise.

The Serengeti was magnificent. When you see a giraffe running in the wild, it blows your mind, and the herds of zebra and wildebeest are a sight to behold. There were thousands of them, but no lions or cheetahs or rhino so far. Hyenas and African dogs sloped around with their arses dragging along behind them. The bus ride was dusty and eventful, highlighted when a couple of bull elephants blocked our way on the road. The Africans were excited, and after the elephants passed, some people got off the bus and collected elephant shit. Apparently, it has a soporific effect when burnt. After the Pyramids, the game parks were my reason to come to Africa, and the Serengeti delivered.

It was about to get better when we arrived at Ngorongoro Crater. We got off the bus near a collection of huts that had staff who administered the protected environment of Ngorongoro and a guest house, which was expensive but worth it. An early rise and a rush to the vehicles that were to transport us down the rim of the crater to the animal paradise below. A Land Rover cost 240 shillings for six passengers—about $2 USD each—and we shared ours with some Americans who were great companions. There was a lake, a plain, and a forest down there for whatever environment the animals needed.

The drivers knew where all the animals were, and we saw rhino, lions, cheetah—every animal you can imagine. They looked healthier than the animals on the plain, where poaching was rife. The baboons were with the elephants, as they always seemed to be, but some charged our Land Rover in a mock attack, which was impressive and scary at the same time.

When it was over, and we came back up, we met a truck/bus full of Americans who were travelling around, and they allowed us to stay with them for the night. We all got stoned, and we decided to sleep underneath the truck for protection against any animals on the prowl. The campsite was fairly exposed, and it was quite cold. There were also a few Masai tribesmen camping nearby, but they remained aloof from us. It was a restless night. I kept fearing being dragged out by a lion or a hyena, who are very daring creatures.

An early rise without breakfast, then a bus trip full of Masai to Arusha, under the shadow of Mt Kilimanjaro. It was a small town with an impressive big tree with pink flowers and hundreds of birds nesting in its branches. I thought about trying to climb Kilimanjaro, but after walking a few hundred meters up the track leading to the top, I realised I did not have the footwear or clothes to do it. I returned to Arusha and caught a bus to Mamanga on the Kenyan border.

Across the border was Masai country—a tall, proud people whose wealth is based on cows. Every relationship has to do with cows. When a girl gets married, cows change hands; when you get thirsty, a cup of milk mixed with cows' blood is the answer. When they celebrate, the men dance and jump. But the most noticeable thing about them is their earlobes. From an early age, their ears are pierced and then widened with a variety of plugs and objects. Some men I saw had to wrap their earlobes many times around their ears to stop them hanging down and getting in the way. I saw many things, including small bottles, in their ears widening the hole—even film canisters. Bizarre.

We bussed to Nairobi in the main form of transport in Kenya—the minibus. We stopped on the way, and I traded an alarm clock and a shirt for a pair of Masai heads carved out of dark wood like ebony. I still have one, and Kris got the other. I have no intention of getting them together again.

The minibus dropped us off on the outskirts of Nairobi, and we walked through the slums, where sewage ran down the middle of the roads, and people with smiling faces lived in ramshackle homes. It was sad to see, but they waved, and nobody accosted us. Once in Nairobi, we checked into the Iqbal Hotel—a hotel that is famous all over the world and a place that most travellers like myself checked into. Downstairs was an African restaurant where you could practice your Swahili with "Chai mbili, asanti sana," or "two teas, thank you." The Kenyans always acted kindly if you spoke in their language. We stayed on the second floor of the Iqbal in a room with 6 or 7 beds and a toilet and shower just outside. We shared it with many travellers, and the atmosphere was brilliant. We were in and out of Nairobi three times, and every time on our return, we looked forward to staying in the Iqbal.

Two Sikh guys used to come to the Iqbal every day to do business that us travellers wanted. They changed money at advantageous rates of 12 shillings per US dollar when the official rate was about 7. They also sold other currencies, and if you wanted bhang, it was always available. This made it cheap to stay here, and we did. Legendary.

As a city, Nairobi had a reputation that we never saw. Many people called it "Nairobbery" because so many people were robbed, particularly at night or in places like City Park. The centre of the city was modern, with Moi Avenue going through the centre and many international hotels. We used the toilets in the international hotels because the outside public ones were full of shit most of the time and totally disgusting. At night, walking around was considered dangerous, but as a group, we felt safe. All the shops had guards outside, many of them Masai carrying the traditional African weapon, the panga or a club. They did smile at us, but we moved quickly. Prostitutes were everywhere, and they had a penchant for using skin-lightening cream on their faces and hands to make themselves look more attractive, I suppose. I was never tempted to use their talents, although I was approached many times.

We had one very strange occurrence when shopping in a market. We were befriended by a wealthy-looking Indian who said he was having some important guests around at his place that night and asked if we would like to come. We said yes, and he took us back to a rather palatial home and said to get cleaned up, and he would be back later. So we did. He had a spa bath, and it was very enjoyable. The night wasn't so good. We met a few European guests, but they were not interested in us, so we had the meal and snuck out to walk back to the city. Nothing lost.

We saw a few movies here, read books, played darts in the international hotels, and bought Scotch eggs for a good price. There was a normality about our life here, and I could easily have stayed, but I was on a mission to get to South Africa and hopefully a boat to Australia from Durban. That was the aim but, alas, not the end result.

I had always wanted to see the source of the Nile and knew it was in Lake Victoria in Uganda, but this country was ruled by a madman called Idi Amin. Weird stories came out about Uganda, but I thought we should give it a crack, so I bought a few Uganda shillings, and we took off in a minibus to Nakuru, where a fabulous lake exists with thousands of flamingos. It was brilliant—all this pink in the middle of the lake. Then, on to Malaba on the Ugandan border. We had heard before we left Nairobi that the British High Commission had been dismissed from Uganda, and it was concerning because if anything went wrong, we had no support in Uganda. I went right up to the border and asked on the Kenyan side how many travellers like myself were crossing into Uganda. He said none, so I decided not to go, and we took a minibus back to Nairobi.

Getting back to Nairobi, the Iqbal was like going home, and it was tempting to get into the easy life. But the mission was still on, so we decided to hitch to Mombasa on the coast and take in Tsavo National Park on the way. On the day we started, there was an airplane crash at Nairobi airport, and that disrupted traffic, but we got a lift with a petrol tanker all the way to Tsavo to see the elephants. We didn't see a lot, and those we did see were all covered in red dust because they picked up the red dirt from the ground and threw it back over their heads onto their bodies. Strange, but I guess it had some use. Back on the road, we got a lift with a Swedish vet who worked at Tsavo and was going into Mombasa. He dropped us off at The Hydro Hotel, where he said travellers went, and we settled into Mombasa. We walked around a large, busy town and met a couple of guys, Bob and Keith, who we had met at the Iqbal. I wanted to change money, so I went with Keith to an international hotel on the beachfront. As we walked in, Rod Stewart came off the beach, spotted us, and said, "Hello, lads. Having a nice time?" We shook his hand, and he carried on to his room. I was staggered.

Twiga Beach was located south of Mombasa—not to be confused with today's resort, which is north. It was a short bus ride from Mombasa, then a 3km walk along a sometimes perilous road to a campground. It had a shop and little else. A truck came every day with supplies at exorbitant prices, and boys often came with melons and other fruit that you could buy cheaply. We took our own supplies and always bought a melon. We slept near a coconut tree and gazed out at the beach and the reef just offshore.

We met many travellers there, and at night there was a bonfire and a party atmosphere. During the day, we walked the beach, played volleyball, and read. We became friends with a group of Canadian lads, and life was sweet. Life could be dangerous along the road in and along the beach, as gangs of armed men sometimes hunted there. One day, a group of campers walked south along the beach to an international hotel some 5kms away. On the way back, they were ambushed by a group of thugs, and to escape, they ran out onto the reef. When they returned, they were scratched and torn and had little spines from starfish embedded in their feet. They reported the incident, but nothing was done. A few days later, we walked the same journey but carried large sticks and made it obvious we meant business. It was a great day drinking by the pool, but the night held a different outcome.

The thing about the tropics is the sun goes down very quickly, and it gets very dark. In the morning, it rises just as quickly and becomes very hot, so there is no lying in bed. The night after our beach walk, we had the usual bonfire, and everybody got stoned and talked shite. One guy walked off, and nobody thought a thing about it. As soon as the sun was up, I did my normal swim in the sea with the Canadian boys, and we found the wanderer's body floating in the sea. We dragged him to shore, and one of our number informed the campground supervisor. The body was very blue, and there was a large gash on the head, looking like it had come from a panga. This was a warning to me; I didn't want to become involved, so we up sticks and walked back to the main road to go back to Mombasa. The road was lined with people, as Jomo Kenyatta, the big chief of Kenya, was driving by with his entourage. We stayed and watched as he waved his fly whisk to the people, then we started walking and were picked up and driven to Mombasa. We needed an entry visa to Tanzania again, settled into the Hydro, and, as luck would have it, we met the Swedish vet who had dropped us off in Mombasa. He was driving to Moshi in Tanzania the next day and offered us a lift, which we accepted with delight.

We got to Moshi, from which Kilimanjaro looks a delight, stayed one night, then caught a bus to the capital Dar es Salaam. It was a spacious city with many beggars and street hawkers and was very expensive. No reason to stay, so we wanted to catch a train south, but nothing was going, even though the Chinese had built a modern rail south. We caught a bus and a two-day ride to Tunduma on the Zambian border. Our aim was to get to the Victoria Falls, cross into Zimbabwe, then on to South Africa very quickly, but things did not go as planned.

Malawi was our first target, and after three changes of bus, two of which broke down, we got to the town of Mzuzu and then onto the lakeside town of Nkhata Bay to get a boat down to a place called Monkey Bay, then on to Lilongwe, the new Malawi capital. Lake Malawi was alleged to be the only African lake without the parasitic snail called Bilharzia, which causes severe intestinal problems and leads to madness. Idi Amin was supposed to have it. So we swam in the lake, slept on the beach, which was stony, and waited five days for the boat to come. It was pleasant living, and we gorged on fresh fish. When the boat came, we encamped around a table with a couple of Americans, Marlene and Mike, and spent two days playing cards and chess while churning down this massive inland sea. We got to Monkey Bay, where there was an international hotel. Marlene and Mike lent us their tent while they stayed in the hotel. They were on their way to New Zealand and did call in on my parents when they visited.

Then it was to Lilongwe, which was very much a new town to be the new capital, but the Malawians were very proud of it. We didn't stay long and made our way quickly to the border town of Chipata, then caught a very modern bus to Lusaka, the capital of Zambia. It was very expensive here and very modern. Sharp-dressed men and women walked the streets, and Afro haircuts were the in thing. We stayed one night, then caught a train to Livingstone, where Stanley said, "Doctor Livingstone, I presume." We planned to cross quickly into Zimbabwe and see the Victoria Falls from there, but it wasn't to be.

After turning up in our best garb, hair combed, and smiling faces, we were declined entry. No reason was given—just a straight "NO," and we were asked to sign a paper to say we agreed with the decision.

"Stick it up your arse," I said, and out we went. The alternative south was to go through Namibia, but the Okavango swamp and river had flooded, and there was no way through. The road was closed, and guerrillas were allegedly in the area. Big decisions had to be made, but first, we went to see the Victoria Falls, and they were majestic. We slept outside in the grounds of an international hotel where the mosquitos were outrageous. Our mosquito net was barely enough to keep them out, and we were bitten badly.

The decision was easy. We decided to make our way back to Kenya, where the cheap flights were, and fly back to England. We then just travelled nonstop on trains and buses back to Nairobi and the Iqbal for the third time, and it was like coming home. But the drama was not over yet.

On New Year's Day 1975, we crossed from Zambia into Tanzania, only to learn that the Tanzania/Kenya border was closed because of a dispute involving Kenyan trucks using Tanzanian roads. Our bus stopped all the time, and a trip that would normally have taken 10 hours stretched to over 30. I wrote in the diary that I took every day and have used to write this African adventure: *"It has been difficult to enjoy travelling in Africa as politically, economically, and socially the whole continent is fucked. The blacks are stupid and corrupt, the whites pig-headed and inferior, and the Asians are the best but barely surviving. Without them, much of the economy would collapse."*

Because of the dispute, Kenyans were going home in droves, and it was almost impossible to get on a bus to Nairobi. We got across the border, and I slipped the bus operator a bribe to get us on the bus, and he did. There was a furious argument that I stayed out of, and we sat in the bus amongst the drama. In the meantime, it was pissing down with rain and was still raining heavily when we got to Nairobi. The Iqbal was full, but we got a couple of beds in Room 4, our favourite, and many of the characters that we met before were still around. Unfortunately, the day we arrived, they closed the downstairs restaurant because of a cholera outbreak, so health was a worry.

For the next seven days, we waited around as Kris was waiting for money to be sent so we could fly to London. It eventually came, and the earliest booking was for 5 February, some two weeks away, so we decided to go to Twiga to pass the time. Hitching to Mombasa proved easy again, and then onto Twiga, where we met the Canadian boys again, who said nothing more was heard about the guy we had pulled dead out of the water weeks earlier.

I used the two weeks to get fit—running, swimming, and exercising every day—then back to Nairobi and the Iqbal for the last time. The flight was in the morning and was very rough. I swear the wing scraped the ground on takeoff, and the thermal currents made the plane shake and bucket up and down. I thought, "Fuck me, how fitting that I should die in an air accident after the ordeal of travel in Africa."

It didn't happen, of course, and on the plane, I wrote my last entry: *"While I have some regrets about leaving Nairobi, I can't wait for London. A change of relationship is definitely needed. Sorry, Africa, but you are just not my scene."*

Snake charmer in Fa'ana square in Marrakesh 1974

Kasbah Quazarzate Morocco 1974.

Roman baths at Carthage Tunisia 1975

Roman Collossium El Djem Tunisia 1974.

Pyramid at Giza taken from halfway up the Cheops. It was scary at the top.

On the deck of ferry to Wadi Halfa in the Sudan.

Top of the rain from Khartoum to Kosti in Sudan.

Rainbow over the Nile on the boat to Juba Sudan 1974.

134

Truck stuck in mud on road to Kissangani Zaire. One of many such stops.

Buying cooked bananas in Zaire. They were delicious.

The sign says it all. Enjoyed the drive through.

A lone zebra. I sometimes felt like this on this trip.

136

Kilimanjaro from the bus window. Not a lot of people know that.

A truck filled with American travelers at Nogorogoro Crater. I slept under it. The best wildlife.

The Iqbal Hotel in Nairobi. The best travelers stop in Africa. My home away from home in Kenya. Istayed in the second floor, window on the right.

Twiga Beach south of Mombasa where some drama happened but lots of fun too. Twiga meansgiraffe in Swahili.

Waiting for the lifeboat to embark the ship to sail to Monkey Bay.
Very risky.

Victoria falls from the Zambian side. Very impressive and as far
south as I got in Africa.

LONDON (February 1975 – July 1975)

On arrival back in London things moved fast because they had to. Kris and I both knew our relationship was over. She got a ticket home and left, and I got a job with an Australian travel company called NATEuro Tours Ltd run by a crafty guy called Warren who had offices in Poland Street and in Earls Court. I went to the interview in my African attire but dazzled them with my knowledge, so they gave me 50 quid to buy a suit and get a haircut and after a little training put me in charge of the Earls Court office called Flight Deck. I was paid 60 quid a week, and they took back their loan over the next few pays.

My job was to sell flights and European tours to Australians mainly, but to anyone who came in the shop. So I did and I was good at it. People would come in every day, and I enjoyed the company. On a Sunday I was expected to accompany a free bus tour to Oxford and Cambridge and sell tours and flights. It was a seven-day-a-week job and I couldn't go and watch West Ham unless there was a mid-week game. I settled into a bedsit in West Kensington and watched TV when I got home. On Friday night after tallying up the books I was expected to go to the rented hotel in Kensington where clients boarded on first arrival in London and do the chat while drinking at the bar. The routine got me down, but then something unexpected happened.

Before the African trip, Kris sent a box of belongings back to Nelson, including some of my things, among which there was an envelope containing marijuana seeds that I got from the Colombian weed I had used in America. I had forgotten about it and had no intention of smuggling it into New Zealand for illicit purposes. But it was found, and Kris was to be charged. I am a reasonable guy, so she asked me to write a letter saying they were mine as it was causing much consternation in her life. So I did. I was not enjoying life, so I decided to go home and managed to wrangle a free flight charged to my employer without their knowledge. On arrival at Christchurch, I was arrested at the airport, charged, searched in all the improper places, and went home to my mother, who was in tears.

EPILOGUE

The privilege of being a Baby Boomer has been a major theme of this memoir to date, and it is fair to say with our music and our attitudes, we had driven huge social change. Men were no longer replicas of their fathers, and women were not their mothers. Our generation had not yet embraced politics in a big way, but the welfare state was still in control of New Zealand, thank heavens for that, and it remained a fairly equitable society without the massive gaps in wealth and opportunities that we have these days. My travels had given me an experience and confidence like nothing else could, and it is very doubtful that my travel exploits could be achieved in the same way by people today.

Certainly, the world is a more dangerous place, and many countries like Iran and Afghanistan are no-go areas for westerners. The big question for me was: could I now go the next step by getting married, buying a house, building a career, and raising a family, or would I keep traveling?

It was a bad start, as I was convicted of possession of marijuana seeds, but fortunately, I didn't need to take my toothbrush to court on the day of my trial. I pleaded guilty with the mitigating circumstance of forgetfulness. I had forgotten they were there, and I admitted the seeds were mine, even though they were in someone else's luggage. I was not a scoundrel. Fortunately, it did not have a major effect on my life from then on, and it has since been expunged from the records.

I got a job as a storeman with the National Film Library, and my boss was one of the finest men I have ever associated with in my life, Norm Roberts. He allowed me rope and understanding that few employers today would have given me. I felt safe and was later able to progress up the ranks, eventually becoming manager of the National Film Library in Auckland and then in Christchurch, my hometown. I ended up doing a Diploma in Library and Information Studies at Victoria University and became a specialist in Children's

Literature at the National Library of NZ. My reviews can still be found on my blog bobsbooksnz.wordpress.com.

I also met the woman who was to become my wife and still is after 49 years: Celia. I fell in love at first sight, and although I was not adept at being a married man and husband, we settled into a small cottage in Holly Road, opposite the Caledonian Hotel, where both our son and daughter were brought into the world. Using the capitalisation of the family benefit and a 3% loan from the Housing Corp, we bought our first home in Ascot Avenue North Beach for the princely sum of $21,000. Tell that to people today, and they are astounded. We lived off one wage and bought a house. You couldn't do that today. I was promoted to manager in Auckland in 1980, and we lived there happily for five years but couldn't afford a house. Auckland properties were going up $1,000 a week even in those days, and only when we returned to Christchurch in 1985 were we able to get back on the property ladder, paying $55,000 for our house, where we still live.

Now, 40 years later, average property values are close to $1m, and even two people working full-time would struggle to buy a house. What the hell has happened to this country? Now that I am retired, Boomers have become derided and ridiculed, and I think that is grossly unfair. The world we grew up in was fair and people-oriented. Not today, where it is profit before people. The world needs to be changed again, but are the current generations able to do that?

I have enjoyed my life, and I hope you have enjoyed reading about my travels. It was fantastic. I now look forward to seeing my granddaughters grow up, but I have to admit I fear they will not have the opportunities that I had.

Cheers,

Robert Docherty

* 9 7 8 1 9 6 6 6 1 7 8 0 8 *